“Because,” Karen said, “you're just like me, Aggie. You can do the same things.”

Aggie refused to hear this. “No, I can't!” she growled. “I'm not like anybody.” This person couldn't possibly know what she was like, what she was going through. What it was like to be her.

“Yes, you are, Aggie,” Karen insisted, still in that soft, gentle voice of hers. “People don't understand you. They don't believe you. They don't know you're not like them. And you can't understand *why* you're not just the same as they are. Things happen on their own when you're around, don't they? Things break, or fly, or just *happen*. And people don't like you because of it. And they don't believe you when you say you've done nothing.”

Aggie stared at the woman in confusion. She was describing some of the things that were really bothering Aggie. But how could she? Was it possible that somebody might actually *listen* to her and believe her? No. She couldn't take that chance. She'd been hurt too much already by rejection. Karen might claim to be on her side right now, but it wouldn't last. It couldn't.

THE OUTER LIMITS™

THE CHOICE

JOHN PEEL

from the television script by
Ann Lewis Hamilton

Tor Kids!
A TOM DOHERTY ASSOCIATES BOOK
NEW YORK

THE OUTER LIMITS #2: THE CHOICE

Cover art by Peter Bollinger

A Tor Book
Published by Tom Doherty Associates, Inc.
175 Fifth Avenue
New York, NY 10010

ISBN: 0-812-59064-3

First edition: September 1997

Printed in the United States of America

0 9 8 7 6 5 4 3 2

For Paul McNamee

It is differences between people that cause conflicts—differences in religion, in race, in language. With differences come dislike and even fear. And fear leads to hatred, and a wish to destroy that which is different. Sometimes such differences become trivial with the passage of time; others seem to force blood to be shed.

Wherever we look in the world, we can see people in conflict because they are different from their neighbors. The Middle East, Africa, Central Europe . . . Wars are fought because the people involved see no other solution but the extermination of those who are different.

And these are wars between two sets of human beings. What wars would be fought if the difference was between two very different species? Between humans . . . and those who will ultimately displace and follow us?

CHAPTER 1

AGGIE TRAVIS STOOD in the playground alone, lost in her own twisted world of trouble. All around her, the other students at the Eugene school were enjoying themselves. Many were playing ball, or other games; some simply stood about, chatting and gossiping, in groups of threes or sixes.

There was a space around Aggie where nobody intruded. Nobody moved to greet her or to play with her. And she didn't seem to be at all bothered by this. Or by anything else. She was alone, as she wanted to be.

It was a normal day.

Why? Aggie raged to herself. *Why is all of this happening to me?* The physical stuff was bad enough; whatever anyone said, going through puberty was never any fun. Her whole body felt wrong and really awkward, and it was doing strange things that made her mostly feel uncomfortable. But at least that was *normal*. Every other girl in her class had gone through it, was enduring it, or would face it soon enough. The boys, too, were experiencing their own changes. That happened to everyone.

It was the *mental* stuff that scared her stupid. As far as she could tell, none of the other students were experiencing anything at all like what she was going through.

Her introspection was cut short as a soccer ball slammed into her left leg, and then rolled to a halt. Aggie stared at it as if it had fallen from a passing flying saucer. Then, realizing what it was, she simply dismissed it from her consideration. It was irrelevant.

But not to others.

The students playing the game had stopped, and one of them snarled, ''Not again!'' Then, ''Hey! Kick it back, you jerk!''

Aggie blinked and looked up.

It was Clark Howell. He was going through his own changes, and they weren't making him any more pleasant. He'd been a tubby, irritating child, and was now losing some of the puppy fat. He was also desperately trying to grow a very thin mustache, and believed that it made him macho. He felt that he had to reinforce this macho image with the rest of the class, to enable him to stay—

''Did you hear me, doofus?'' he demanded.

Aggie blinked again. *How do I know with such certainty what worries him?* she wondered. Another thing to worry about . . . ''I am not a doofus,'' she said very clearly. ''Nor am I a jerk.''

Clark sniggered. ''You are, too,'' he replied. He moved forward slightly. Some of the other players joined him.

Aggie shook her head. She refused to accept his insults. *He's only doing it because you scare him,* she told herself. *He's unsure of you, insecure, and he needs to maintain his so-called dignity. So he picks on you.* Aggie blinked again.

Stop that! she screamed to herself. She didn't want to know any of that. She just wanted to be left in peace—by Clark, by the other kids . . . and mostly by her own self. She stared at Clark, focusing in on him as her problem at the moment. "Take it back," she demanded. *You're only making matters worse,* that horrible Voice in her head informed her. *He's with his friends; he won't back down, you know.*

Moving closer, Clark gave a nasty grin. "Okay," he agreed, surprisingly. "You're not a jerk or a doofus." He grinned at his companions. "You're pond scum." He laughed, and several of his friends joined in.

Told you so, the inner Voice said smugly. *This means trouble . . .* Aggie refused to listen, but she couldn't help hearing the unpleasant laughter of the other kids around her. They'd circled her now, laughing, with nasty, mean thoughts in their minds and on their faces. *They don't like you,* the Voice in her head told Aggie. *Well, I don't like them,* Aggie snapped back at it. *I don't care.*

Clark's hand suddenly shot out and slapped her shoulder. "Pond scum," he jeered. "Pond scum!" He slapped at her again.

"Leave me alone!" Aggie yelled, backing up a pace. But there were people behind her, too, and one of them shoved at her, making her stumble back to where Clark's rough hand caught her again. "Leave me alone!"

"Make us," Clark sneered, punching harder at her arm this time.

Aggie was worried and bewildered. Why wouldn't they just let her be? She wasn't hurting them. She was only hurting herself. Her arm felt as if it were being bruised. Emboldened by Clark's attack on her, a couple of other kids were smacking her about the arms and back, some of them not too gently.

This was too much for Aggie to take. Anger burst out into her body, and she wanted nothing more than to strike back at them all. "I hate you!" she snarled. "I hate you all!" Her face was flushed with anger, embarrassment, and other emotions too confusing to be able to define. Deep inside her, something seemed to twist.

And the world changed.

Luckily, this time Aggie was too angry to be scared of what she now saw. It was as if she'd somehow twisted reality sideways, and was looking at it from a totally different perspective. The first time this had happened, it had terrified her. She'd thought she was going blind, or having a brain tumor, or something. Now, though, it was simply something that she could do.

People looked different. Instead of being solid, they were sort of vague. And a brilliant halo of light shone around their bodies. It was a bit like an infrared photo she'd seen once in geography class, where heat from living creatures showed up brightly colored. The aura of light about each child was subtly different, and Aggie knew that all of the colors *meant* something. But it was like listening to people talking to one another in a foreign language—you know they're making sense, but it's all so much gibberish to you. Aggie knew that the halos of pulsing light about each person *meant* something; she simply had no idea *what*.

But there was one thing she had figured out. She had a halo of her own, though it was pretty much invisible to her. It had to be, or she wouldn't have been able to see out past it. But she could use that halo, as if it were a hand or a fist, to affect things.

And while she was angry, she didn't care if anyone saw her do it, or knew. Flailing out with her fists at her tormentors was futile. They were all able to laugh and jeer and step out of her way.

But they couldn't avoid what she did using her light.

A tentacle of brightness shot out from her head, and

slammed into the aura about Clark. He gave a howl of pain, and there was a splash of redness in his halo that hadn't been there before. She struck out, again and again, and the tentacle skipped from one person to another, always leaving that blotch of red.

Suddenly, the blows on her back and shoulders stopped, and Aggie realized that the other students were moving away from her. *They're afraid*, the Voice inside her said. *They don't know what is happening. Only that you're hurting them somehow.* Aggie grinned to herself. *Good,* she told the Voice. *That's what I wanted to do. They deserve to be hurt. All I want them to do is to leave me alone.*

Her anger started to die down, and as it did, her vision cleared, and she could see the real world once again. She blinked furiously, hardly able to understand what she was seeing.

Clark's nose was bleeding all down his front. He was howling, and trying to stop the flow with a wadded-up tissue, but without much luck. Megan Sikowski had a long scratch down the side of her face that dripped blood over her fingers. She looked as if she were in shock, staring at Aggie. Donnie Winters had a bright stain on his sleeve, and he was clutching his arm in pain. Karen Danvers had a huge bruise on her upper arm, just below the sleeve of her T-shirt, and tears in her eyes.

Had she done all that? Aggie was amazed, and simply stared at them. They stared back, obviously frightened and lacking any understanding of what had just taken place.

Miss Myers came running across the playground, breathless and shocked. "What did you do, Aggie?" she cried, staring at the silent students.

"Nothing!" Aggie protested. "I didn't do anything! They just—"

"That's quite enough, young lady," Miss Myers said firmly, taking hold of her shoulder. "You can come with me."

She looked at Clark and the others. "You'd better all go in and see the nurse. Move!" As they started to hurry toward the school building, the teacher glared down at Aggie. "Little savage," she muttered. "You're in for it this time, I can promise you."

"But it wasn't *me*!" Aggie protested. She allowed herself to be dragged along. "It's not fair! I didn't do anything."

Miss Myers snorted angrily. "I don't think anyone will believe that this time, Aggie Travis," she snapped. "You've gone too far this time. It's high time you were punished."

There was absolutely no point in protesting any further. Aggie could see that. *She thinks you're a bully,* the inner Voice informed her. *Disruptive and disgraceful. She wants you expelled from school.*

Aggie felt a numbness inside her. The previous complaints had been bad enough. How was she ever going to explain any of this to her parents?

As if they ever listened to *her* side of things!

This, she knew, meant the worst kind of trouble. . . .

CHAPTER 2

IT WAS AMAZING *how sitting in the principal's office made you feel guilty,* Leslie Travis thought. Here she was, thirty-four years old, and an art director at a design firm, drawing good money, and she felt as if she were thirteen again, back in school and called out on the carpet for some minor infraction of the rules. The fact that she was here because of her daughter's actions didn't help relieve the guilt at all.

Mrs. Whelan steepled her hands and stared at Leslie and her husband, Joe. There was something about principals, too, that made them all look alike. Pleasant faces that could transform in an instant to the Disapproving Frown. Mrs. Whelan's face wore the Frown right now. Leslie ran her hand through her short, dark hair nervously, then caught herself and stopped.

''This is the fifth incident in as many weeks,'' Mrs. Whelan said. ''One girl claims she was pushed over in the playground.

Another, that Agatha dropped books on her head. One of her classrooms looked like a Tasmanian devil had gone on a rampage in it. And, as always, Agatha claims that she didn't do anything.''

Oh dear . . . the same old story. ''We know Aggie has some emotional problems,'' Leslie admitted, wringing her hands together. ''We're looking for a new therapist.'' No point in saying why they *needed* a new therapist! ''But the other children pick on her and she just gets so frustrated.''

Leaning forward, Joe added, ''She'll get better. If you could just give her one more chance . . .'' His voice trailed off under the withering Disapproving Frown.

''Mr. Travis,'' Mrs. Whelan said firmly, ''the problem is the other parents. I've had several complaints that we're putting their children in an unsafe environment. The school lawyers assure me that we would be legally liable if any of the children were seriously hurt and the parents chose to sue. Believe me, I understand how you feel. But I simply have no choice in the matter. I must insist that Aggie be removed from the school and transferred to one which deals with children of . . . special needs.''

''Special needs?'' echoed Leslie, a sinking feeling in her stomach. She knew what that polite term meant. ''My daughter is *not* retarded!''

''No one is saying that she is,'' Mrs. Whelan replied, clearly bothered by the conversation. ''On the contrary, she's an excellent pupil with a fine mind. If it weren't for her behavioral problem, I would be recommending advancing her a grade. But that is precisely the point: her behavior is disruptive and uncontrollable and . . .'' Her voice faded out.

''And *what*?'' demanded Joe, leaning forward, annoyed.

''Dangerous,'' Mrs. Whelan finally finished.

Joe slammed his hand down on the principal's desk. ''That's ridiculous!'' he exclaimed. ''I know that Aggie has problems, maybe makes a mess now and then, but she would never hurt anyone!''

''Clark Howell didn't hit *himself* on the nose,'' Mrs. Whelan pointed out, refusing to give an inch.

''And Aggie insists she never touched him,'' Leslie replied. ''Maybe it was one of the other kids? They *were* ganging up on her, and they might have hit one another by mistake.''

Mrs. Whelan shook her head slowly. ''There were eight other children involved in the incident. They all maintain that Agatha was the one who inflicted the injuries. Only your daughter claims her innocence.''

''As if *they'd* admit to being in the wrong,'' Leslie scoffed.

''I'm sorry,'' Mrs. Whelan said. ''But my decision is final. Agatha must be withdrawn from this school and sent to a special school.'' Her ferocious frown broke slightly. ''She'll be better off there in the long run. They have specialized teachers there who may be able to get through to her and discover why she's behaving the way that she is. They are more likely to help her.''

''Help her?'' Leslie was furious. ''You're branding my child as developmentally backward and you try to pretend that's *helping* her?''

''I'm sorry you feel like this,'' the principal replied. ''But in time, I'm sure you'll agree it's for the best.''

''No,'' Leslie snapped. ''No, I'll *never* see that. You can't do this to my child!''

''The decision is made,'' Mrs. Whelan said firmly.

Joe jumped to his feet. ''Is it?'' he growled. ''Well, the other parents aren't the only ones who can file a lawsuit against this school, you know, as you'll discover first thing tomorrow morning, I promise you!'' He whirled around and marched toward the door.

With a last, angry look at the unrepentant principal, Leslie followed him. Outside, Aggie sat waiting. From the distressed expression on her face, she must have somehow overheard what had been said. Well, voices had been raised . . .

"Come along, sweetheart," Leslie said, trying to control her anger. "We're leaving this place right now." Aggie simply nodded, and joined her parents as they stormed out of the school.

Joe led the way to the family car, and clambered into the front passenger seat. "You drive," he ordered Leslie. "I'm going to call Alan right now." Snatching up the car phone, he dialed their lawyer's number. Aggie slipped into the back seat, her expression unreadable again.

Starting the car, Leslie gave a last, furious look at the school building. They'd pay for what they'd just done. There was nothing wrong with her daughter—nothing!

Well . . . maybe not *nothing*, but it wasn't what Mrs. Whelan had suggested. Aggie wasn't retarded. She was just . . . well, a little *different*, that was all. Leslie remembered her own school days; anyone different was a target for the insecure bullies. Like that Clark What's-his-name. The *nerve* of that Whelan woman, blaming Aggie for all of this!

Later that night, Leslie almost collapsed in the bedroom. The strain of the day had taken its toll on her, and her nerves were raw. Joe had arranged to start a lawsuit with Alan, but their attorney hadn't been very hopeful.

"By the time this is even heard," he had pointed out, "months will pass. Aggie will have to go to the special school in the meantime. Once she's been there a while, she'll find going back to regular school almost impossible." He'd come around in person to show them the papers. "The other kids appear to be picking on her now; you can just imagine what their behavior will be like if she's been in a special school for several months."

"I don't care," Leslie had said. "I'm not going to let her

be branded like this. You know she'll never get into college with something like this on her record. That school is trying to ruin her life!''

''Well, I'll file,'' Alan had replied, gathering up the signed forms. ''But it's not going to be over all that soon, you know. And the school is bound to fight back. They have to, to cover themselves. They're going to throw every bit of mud that they can at Aggie in court, in the hopes that some of it will stick. You're going to be subjecting Aggie to some ferocious cross-examination that won't be very easy on her.''

''So what are you saying?'' Joe had asked. ''That we should just give up and go with it? Let them wreck Aggie's life for her?''

''No, of course not. But I don't want you to think that this will be easy. It's going to be very hard on both of you. And it'll be hardest of all on Aggie herself.''

Leslie couldn't get all this out of her mind as she got ready for bed. It was like living in a nightmare, where you have to escape some terrible danger, only to discover you're moving at the speed of a sloth stuck in molasses. She'd known that there was a problem with Aggie for a while, but it had never occurred to her that anything like this could happen.

Aggie's a good girl at heart, she thought to herself. *It's just that . . . well, something seems to have happened to her these past couple of months. Maybe it's the puberty thing. . . .* She remembered how awkward she herself had felt at the changes taking place within her body. It had been so difficult to cope sometimes. But she'd never gone off the deep end, as Aggie had. So why was Aggie taking things so hard?

Joe rubbed her tense neck, taking away a little—but very little—of the strain. ''Has she gone to bed?'' he asked.

''Almost.'' Leslie sighed. ''It's so hard, Joe. She won't *talk* to me. I know she's hurting, but I don't know *why.*''

''It's the same with me,'' her husband admitted. ''A big

wall between us, and a blank stare to every question I ask.''

''This . . . these aren't simply normal problems,'' Leslie said reluctantly. She hated to even voice the thought, but it had to be stated. If it was left hidden, it would simply fester in all of their minds. ''She can't understand why I find it so hard to believe her. I think she really feels like we're betraying her. Joe, what are we going to do with her?'' She looked up at him in despair, and saw that there was little hope in his eyes, too.

Aggie was ready for bed, but she had no intention of going there right away. Quickly, her bare feet making no noise on the carpet, she slipped into her parents' bathroom. The toilet seat was up, so she gently lowered it and sat on it, and closed her eyes.

The walls were thin, and she could hear every word her parents were saying. She didn't need that sneaky Voice to tell her what was going on right now. They were talking about her, of course. She had known that they must be. And she wanted to hear what they would never say in front of her.

''I don't know, honey,'' her father said, answering her mother's question of what they were going to do with Aggie. ''Right now, we have no real option but to send her to that *special* school.'' He said the word as if it were a plague. ''But we can't make her suffer for that long.''

''No,'' her mother said firmly. ''It would ruin her chances of getting into college. Oh, Joe, I have such dreams for Aggie. She's so bright, she could be almost anything she wants to be. If only . . .''

''If only she didn't have this behavioral problem,'' her father finished. ''But she *does*, honey, and we have to deal with it.''

''How?'' Her mother sounded close to despair. ''The analysts don't seem to be working. Dr. Hammer won't even allow her in his office again after her last tantrum."

"Maybe what Aggie needs is some quality attention," her father said slowly.

"You think she doesn't get that from *us*?" demanded her mother angrily.

"Of course she does, hon. But . . . well, maybe *we're* part of her problem. She seems to think we don't believe in her."

That's because you don't, Aggie thought to herself. *You've never asked me what I want. You've just told me what's best for me. In your opinion.*

"Then what do you mean?" Her mother sounded puzzled, but hopeful.

"We could try an at-home tutor," her father suggested. "Someone who's used to dealing with . . . difficult children. Someone who can take some of the burden off us."

Burden? Aggie thought, appalled. *Is that what they see me as—a burden? And a "difficult child"?* She couldn't help herself: the anger inside her was starting to grow . . .

"Somebody at work told me about a new agency," her father continued, oblivious to the fact that Aggie could hear his every word. "They'd heard that we were having problems, and they slipped me this business card. Maybe I could give them a call and just see . . ."

Her mother sounded worried now. "Joe, we can't afford that. We're both already working, and we don't have much saved up."

"I can put in more hours," her father said gently, persuasively. "I've already spoken to Frank about it. And there's always the possibility of getting a grant. Besides," he added, bitterness tingeing his voice, "right now, I really don't think we have much of a choice."

The anger inside Aggie was burning at her mind. They were planning on dumping her on some old bat of a tutor, so that they wouldn't have to deal with her problems any longer! As if they'd managed to deal with her so far! She'd *tried* to talk to them, to somehow explain what was happening to her. But they simply hadn't been able to believe her. They'd heard her explain about the lights she saw about people, and they'd thought she was hallucinating.

They wouldn't believe her. They wouldn't accept her. They wouldn't help her.

They just wanted her off their hands, problem solved. . . .

"But what if that doesn't work either?" asked her mother. "I mean, even if we can find the right someone to be her tutor, how long do you think we'd be able to keep them? With a little girl who hurts other kids, and who lies all the time?"

Aggie's face was getting red, and she stopped trying to control her anger. If that's what they thought of her . . .

The medicine cabinet on the wall started to rattle.

"We don't know that she lies," her father argued weakly.

"Oh, come on, Joe!" her mother snapped. "Things around her break, but Aggie always claims that she didn't do it. Someone gets a bloody nose—but she didn't do it. The fish tank shatters—but she didn't do it."

Her father gave up the unequal fight. "Let's burn that bridge when we come to it," he suggested, a weak joke to try to appease her mother.

It didn't appease Aggie.

The anger broke, and she couldn't control herself. Colors lashed all about her, touching and slapping everything in the room.

The medicine cabinet rattled on the wall, and the door flew open. Tablets rained down as bottle tops swirled open and away. Bottles fell, shattering before they hit anything. A can of shaving cream exploded into action, spraying the room in lather.

Aggie paid attention to none of it, even when liquid or foam splashed and sprayed over her nightie. Furious, she simply sat on the toilet seat, allowing the waves of rage to do as they willed. She didn't even hear her mother's cry: "What the hell is *that*?"

And then the door burst open, and her parents stood in the doorway. They stared at the room at first in shock, and then in anger.

"Aggie!" her father demanded. "What's going on?"

The colored lights had stopped whirling, and everything was back to normal again. Aggie blinked furiously and then managed to focus on the room.

It was a dreadful mess. Pools of cough syrup and other goo had splattered the sink and floor. The shaving cream had left white, whipped lines all over the walls, floor, and ceiling. Headache pills, allergy pills, and who knew what else were rattling about in the sink, or rolling across the floor. Even the toilet paper had burst from its holder and sprayed all around the room.

And she herself was covered in all kinds of stuff. Brushing the hair back out of her eyes gingerly, so as not to get cough syrup in it, she said quietly, "Everything just started shaking."

"By itself?" her father exclaimed, stunned. "Look at this mess, Aggie!" He shook his head, clearly having a hard time keeping his temper locked in. "This is going to stop! Do you hear me?" He grabbed her shoulders in his large hands and shook her angrily.

Aggie was too confused to know what to do. Her father had never hurt her in her life. He didn't believe in hitting a child. But she could sense in his face that he was very close to breaking that belief.

"Joe!" her mother exclaimed. "What are you doing?"

Her father blinked, and forced himself very obviously to calm down. Aggie could feel the tension in his hands, and then he slowly opened them, letting her go free. She glared up at him, hurt by this latest betrayal. ''I don't know why this happened,'' she told them both. ''It just did! Why won't you simply believe me?'' Then, hurting too much, she ran from the room.

''I'm sorry,'' she heard her father say. ''I never did that before. It's just . . .''

Aggie didn't care what it was *just*. She'd been betrayed again. They jumped to conclusions, and simply assumed she was lying to them. They wouldn't listen to her at all. *Nobody* would listen to her. Nobody would believe her. There was no one she could turn to, no one she could trust.

She went into her own bathroom and stripped off her filthy nightie. Washing the goo off her hands and face, she donned a fresh robe, and stalked into her room.

Her mother was there, waiting. She had one of those I'm-here-to-be-your-friend faces on. It was another lie, of course. She was here only to twist the knife a little further into Aggie's heart.

''Aggie,'' she said gently, ''you have to forgive your father. It's such a stress on him right now, and—''

''I don't care,'' Aggie said, making a mask of her face again. She slid into bed. ''I know he's angry with me. And I know you are, too.''

''We're not *angry*,'' her mother denied. Aggie simply looked at her in total disbelief. ''Well, maybe we're a *little* angry,'' her mother conceded. ''But mostly we're just worried. Why do you do these things? Like in the bathroom just now?''

''I didn't do *anything*,'' Aggie said, fighting back her own anger and frustration. ''I just sat there. Everything simply fell over. I didn't touch anything.'' She looked up at her mother. ''Why won't you believe me?'' she asked. ''You always just assume I'm lying. Why can't you trust me?''

"Because what you're saying makes no sense," her mother replied. "Things don't just *happen*. There's always a cause for them. And you're always the only one around when these things happen. What else are we to believe?"

"Believe *me*!" Aggie cried.

But it was hopeless. Her mother shook her head. "We'll talk about this some more in the morning," she decided. "We'll have calmed down by then, and maybe you'll realize that the best thing you can do is to tell the truth for once." She kissed Aggie automatically on the forehead, and then left the room.

Hurt, betrayed, and depressed, Aggie sank back in her bed. Why did she even bother trying? They *never* listened to her. They never believed her. And things wouldn't be any better in the morning. The more she told the truth, the angrier they always became. And now she had to go to a school for problem kids. She knew she wasn't going to like that. And the other alternative, some kind of tutor—that sounded even worse.

Her parents were just trying to avoid having to listen to her. Anything but that.

Aggie drifted into a cold, betrayed sleep, feeling abandoned and unwanted.

CHAPTER 3

RUTH DAVIES HAD always enjoyed working at Antiquarius Books. It was a cluttered sort of place on two levels, with an old, winding stairway connecting both. Everywhere in the store were large cases filled with used books. The ones upstairs were the valuable ones—the first editions, the signed copies, the foreign books. Down below were the popular novels, the used paperbacks and the old magazines. There was something really pleasant about working with books that suited Ruth's temperament.

Besides, the store was a wonderful cover for their *real* activities. Who would ever suspect a slightly fusty little shop like this of hiding any secrets at all?

Ruth made her way through the aisles of books to the front counter. It was almost opening time, and Jean Anderson insisted on punctuality, even though there was never a mad rush by customers dying to get inside. Jean didn't care: she was one of those grim, methodical people who insisted on everything being done just so, and accepted no deviations. Ruth was more of a free spirit, preferring to let things drift as they would. She had to constantly curb this attitude whenever Jean was present.

As she was today. She was at the corner desk, working on the computer. Whenever customers came in, Jean would be reading through *Books in Print* on a disk, ostensibly looking for a ''special order'' that didn't exist. Her real work lay hidden while there were outside eyes to spy. Jean was in her early sixties, though she looked a decade younger and acted a quarter of a century younger still. She was filled with energy and determination, and an unswerving dedication to her work. Which was not books. If it weren't for Ruth, the place would be impossible. As it was, Antiquarius Books wasn't simply a front, it was also a moderately successful small business.

A glint of light caught on the crystal around Jean's neck. On a thin gold chain, the thumb-sized green crystal glittered in the ray of sunshine before Jean bent her head and it vanished into shadow again. Ruth fingered the twin of that crystal that hung about her own neck, and glanced at the clock. Ten minutes to opening time. . . .

The phone rang. Ruth scooped it up, and said, pleasant and upbeat, ''Antiquarius Books.''

The person at the other end of the line said good morning, and inquired about the new Margaret Atwood novel.

Ruth couldn't remember. She'd sent in the order, she knew, but when was it due? Covering the phone, she called out, ''Jean, have we got any paperback copies of the new Margaret Atwood yet?''

Without pausing in her work, Jean replied, ''They're due in in the next shipment tomorrow.''

Ruth smiled, and then answered the caller, ''Check with us again on Friday, why don't you? We should have them in by then.'' The man on the phone thanked her and rang off. Ruth hesitated a moment, and then replaced the receiver. "I don't know how you do it," she commented.

"Do what?" asked Jean. She was opening envelopes, none of which contained book orders or queries. Most contained only newspaper clippings, carefully dated and identified by town and state.

Joining her at the desk, Ruth nodded down. "Keep all our orders in your head at the same time you're reading all these. And being on the computer." She picked up one clipping that Jean had picked out and looked at it. The person who'd sent it had written *"Eugene, Oregon"* and Monday's date on it. There was a small headline: "Parents Sue School Board Over Child Expulsion." It ran just a few paragraphs, obviously simply filler in a local paper.

Without looking up, Jean took the clipping back, and set it on a clipboard by the computer. She was still scanning another clipping, which she then tossed into the wastebasket. "I guess I've always been able to . . . shift mental gears," she replied, distracted.

"You should try to teach a course in it," Ruth joked. She picked up a stack of books from one of the last boxes to have arrived. A display of these Ed McBains wouldn't hurt sales.

"Maybe I will one day," Jean said vaguely. She picked up the telephone and dialed a number from memory. It rang several times before a sleepy voice replied.

"Hello, it's Jean," she said. "I've got another target for you."

Ruth started working on the display. She couldn't hear the other end of the conversation, but she could hear everything Jean was saying.

"I know you just came in, and I'm sorry about it," she said. She certainly didn't sound sorry; she was in her work mode now. Somehow, something in that clipping had sparked her interest. "Rachel and Sarah are already on assignments, and I simply can't pull them out when they're so close to their objectives. It has to be you.'' There was a short pause. ''Good. I knew I could rely on you. The location is Eugene, and the family's name is Travis. They're looking for a tutor for their daughter, so I hope you can fake up some credentials without trouble. I'll E-mail you all the details. I'm sorry that you've not had much chance to rest, but it's essential that you move immediately. We can't allow this one to escape.''

Aggie lay in her room, her eyes closed, focusing on as little as possible. The first few days at the special school had been a nightmare. She certainly wasn't looking forward to spending the rest of her school years there. Even though she was eleven, she had dug out one of her old dolls and hugged it tightly against her chest. She needed a friend more than anything else in the world right now, and if there wasn't a human being who'd be that friend, then an old doll would have to do. When she was seven, she'd thought they were all real personalities, and had talked to them for hours. She didn't believe that they were real anymore, of course, but at least when she talked to them, they didn't accuse her of being a liar.

''It's not the school's fault,'' she told the doll. ''I mean, they *try*. The teachers are kind of nice, actually. They seem sympathetic. But they're overworked, looking after the children with *real* problems. They don't have any time for me at all.'' And that was true. She was in a small class of only ten children, and there was a teacher and an assistant. That was a big difference from her old school, where there were thirty kids to one teacher. But the other students had worse problems than she did.

There was one child who was subject to fits. Aggie hadn't seen her actually throw any, but the teachers always acted like the child was a volcano, ready to erupt at any second. There were two who were autistic, and didn't want to communicate at all. Even the Voice in Aggie's mind couldn't get through to them; they were lost in their own private universe. And then . . .

"But why go on?" she asked the doll. Naturally, there was no answer. "They just assume I'm dumb, or something. The lessons aren't *real* lessons. I'm never going to learn anything there. It's like a day care center for kids nobody else wants." Aggie understood that the teachers were filled with compassion for their charges and were doing their best. But she simply didn't belong there, whatever Mrs. Whelan believed.

"There's got to be something better," Aggie confided in the doll. "My life's a total misery right now. It couldn't possibly get any worse, not even if this tutor Mom and Dad are talking about turns out to be a stupid old bat with thick glasses, a hearing aid and clothes made in the last century. There's just no way my life could get any worse right now." A tear trickled down her cheek. This was the pits. It couldn't possibly get worse.

"Ms. Ross?"

Karen Ross peered through her spectacles at the young woman at her door. "Yes," she confirmed, wondering what this was about. The woman was barely more than a girl, sort of hippie-looking. She had long, dusty-blond hair that hung straight, halfway down her back. She wore a long skirt and laced boots, and a floral print blouse. She had a backpack slung over one shoulder. There were touches of a tan about her pretty face, and her cheery smile showed white teeth.

"Oh, hi." The girl held out her hand. "I'm Leslie Travis."

"Leslie . . . ?" Ms. Ross scowled down at her, and then reluctantly moved aside to allow the young woman to enter her house. "I was under the impression that it was I who was to come and see you—later this afternoon."

"That was the original plan, yes," Mrs. Travis replied, with another of her cheery smiles. "But something came up, and I thought I'd better see you in person."

The house was immaculate, of course, as always, so Ms. Ross didn't mind having a visitor in. Truth be told, she had precious few visitors, and a young person brightened the house a little. Then she frowned, puzzled. "Forgive me for saying this, Mrs. Travis, but I was under the impression that the child, Agatha, is eleven years old. You don't look old enough to have an eleven-year-old daughter."

The young woman grinned again. "Thanks for the compliment," she answered. "Actually, I'm a little older than I look, but you're right. Agatha is Mr. Travis's daughter by his first wife. I've only been Mrs. Travis for a year and a half."

"Oh, I see." Ms. Ross pursed her mouth. "It would have been helpful of you to have included that information in the application that you sent me. It's often the case that a child is deeply disturbed by her parents' divorce. It may provide a key to understanding Agatha's attitude problems. Really, how can I be expected to do my job properly if no one *tells* me these things?"

"I'm sorry, Ms. Ross," Mrs. Travis apologized. "But, as it happens, something has changed matters." She was playing with a little crystal on a gold chain that hung around her neck. It was like one of those silly New Age things you could buy at gift shops in the mall. But it was oddly attractive, somehow, the way that the sunlight played upon its facets. . . .

"You like my crystal?" the young woman asked.

She had such a pleasant, low-pitched voice. No wonder Mr. Travis had left his first wife for this girl. She could get just about anything she wanted with her looks and a voice like that. Ms. Ross found herself nodding, unable to draw her attention away from the crystal.

"Good," Mrs. Travis purred. "Keep watching the crystal, Karen, and listen to what I'm telling you. You will believe everything I say. There is no need to check anything. Do you understand?''

Ms. Ross nodded slowly, her eyes still drawn to the multitude of lights in the crystal. ''Of course.''

''Good,'' the young woman said. ''There is no need for you to go to the Travis house. The job has already been taken. You feel perfectly happy about that. Young Agatha is getting wonderful care. You will forget all about the job after today, because everything is fine, isn't it?''

''Of course it is,'' she agreed dreamily. What a silly question! Any fool could tell that Agatha was in good hands. Why should she be at all worried? Everything was fine.

''Good,'' Mrs. Travis said. ''Now, let me see your credentials, Karen, if you'd be so kind.''

''Of course,'' Ms. Ross said amiably. There was no problem with showing this lovely young lady anything. She fished the laminated card out of her bag and handed it across to Mrs. Travis. ''Here you are.''

''Thank you.'' The young woman took the card and studied it carefully. ''The picture should be simple enough to replace,'' she murmured to herself. Tucking the card into her own bag, she said gently, ''Tomorrow, you'll discover that you've misplaced your card. You'll simply have to get yourself a new one, won't you?''

''Certainly,'' Ms. Ross agreed. That would be no problem at all. Silly of her to lose her card, really. She wasn't normally as clumsy as that. Perhaps she *was* getting a trifle old, after all. She was *almost* sure she'd seen it quite recently, too.

''Right, then,'' Mrs. Travis said. ''You look a little tired, you know. Perhaps you should lie down and rest for a while. After all, since the job's been filled, you won't be going anywhere for a few hours, will you? So just relax, and sleep. You deserve some peace. I'll just let myself out so that I don't disturb you.''

"How very thoughtful," murmured Ms. Ross. "Now that you mention it, I do feel a trifle fatigued. Perhaps just a short rest . . ."

"That's the spirit, Karen," the young woman said. "You'll really enjoy a good rest. And when you wake up, you'll know that everything is all right, won't you? And tomorrow you'll forget all about the Travis family and their little problems, because they're all solved now. Sleep . . ."

Ms. Ross lowered herself onto the couch, and everything went delightfully dreamy. . . .

When the doorbell rang, Leslie rushed to answer it. This had to be that tutor! She could only pray that she'd be what Aggie needed. She knew what that special school was doing to Aggie's spirits—and her chance of ever getting into Wellesley. She opened the door, and frowned down at the young woman who stood there. "Yes?" she asked politely, studying her. She was dressed in rather retro fashion—a long skirt, a floral print shirt and lace-up boots. She had long off-blond hair that hung down to the middle of her back, and a very pretty face that was immediately lit by a high-voltage smile.

"Mrs. Travis?" she asked, holding out a slender hand. "Hi. I'm Karen Ross. The new tutor."

CHAPTER 4

"OH." LESLIE SMILED at the young woman. "Do come in." She moved out of the doorway, and Karen stepped inside, lowering a backpack into her hands. "Ah . . . forgive me for saying this," Leslie went on, "but you seem a little . . . young to be a tutor."

Karen gave her another of those lovely smiles. "Thanks for the compliment," she answered. "Actually, I'm a little older than I look. And I assure you that I do have good credentials."

"Oh, I'm sure you do." Leslie was glad she hadn't offended the young woman. But there was that feeling of wrongness still in her mind. Maybe she was just reacting to stereotypes. Seeing tutors as stern old ladies. There was something immensely likable about Karen Ross. She led the woman into the main room, where Joe was waiting, and introduced them to each other.

Joe frowned slightly, and commented, "I was expecting someone a little . . ."

"Older?" Karen finished for him, putting her backpack on the floor and accepting the offered chair.

He flushed a little. "Well, yes, frankly."

"Then I hope I'm not a disappointment," Karen replied. "Your girl is what? Eleven? Now, a grandmotherly figure is all well and good, but Agatha is apparently having troubles of an emotional nature. My agency believes that she's more likely to open up to someone who has the energy and stamina to keep up with her, so we tend to use young women. But that doesn't mean that we skimp on the qualifications." She grimaced. "Trust me, I've been through more tests and examinations than you'd ever want to take."

"I see," Joe said slowly. Leslie reached over and squeezed his hand.

"It sounds pretty reasonable to me," she said softly.

"And you can always see how it goes," Karen added. "If, after a trial period, you don't feel I'm doing Agatha any good, then all you have to do is request that I be replaced. By someone much older, if that's your wish. But at least give our methods a try first, Mr. and Mrs. Travis, before you decide against them."

Joe nodded. "That's very reasonable," he agreed.

Leslie smiled. "I think so. By the way, she prefers to be called Aggie."

"Right." Karen smiled again. "I'm from a large family myself, and I love children. I'm sure Aggie and I will get along just fine."

"How big is your family?" Joe asked.

"There are eight of us," Karen told him. "I'm the eldest, so I helped out a lot. That's how it goes in large families. Now, you have only Aggie?"

"Yes," Leslie replied. "And we have to tell you . . ." She caught the warning glance that Joe shot her, but she ignored it. It wouldn't be fair to go into this arrangement by hiding information from the tutor. ''There have been some problems.''

Karen nodded sympathetically. ''Of course. Exactly what kind of problems?''

Taking a deep breath and not looking at Joe, Leslie continued, ''Aggie is a little . . .'' She groped for the right word. ''At first, the doctors thought it was attention deficit disorder.''

''At first?'' Karen probed gently.

''It could be worse than that,'' admitted Leslie.

''She just gets a little . . .'' Joe added, also trying to find a good but neutral word for it. ''There have been . . . incidents at school. With the other kids.''

''And sometimes she breaks things,'' added Leslie.

''Breaks things?'' Karen seemed to be professionally detached. ''What sorts of things?''

''Her toys,'' Leslie explained. ''Sometimes dishes. Those kinds of things.'' She looked to Joe for help, but he scowled, obviously afraid that Karen would decide against taking Aggie on.

''But she's a very sweet girl really,'' he said, a trifle lamely.

Karen smiled again, all sunshine once more. ''I'm sure she is. I'd really like to meet her.''

''Fine.'' Joe rose and left the room.

Leslie turned back to Karen. ''Ah, you said something about credentials?'' she prompted, not wanting to upset the young woman by prying.

''Right,'' Karen agreed. She opened her purse and handed over a card. ''That's my ID.'' Leslie glanced at it while Karen fished in her backpack. It was from the state Board of Education, and had Karen's picture on it and her signature, plus the authorization of the state of Oregon. She handed it back as Karen gave her a large, thin envelope.

''The phone number and report from the Board of Education are in there,'' she explained. ''You can call them up at any time and check everything out.'' She grinned. ''Don't worry, I won't be offended. It just makes good sense.''

''Thanks.'' Leslie smiled back at her. She had liked Karen from the start, and she seemed to be so understanding and cheery. Maybe she was *exactly* what Aggie needed. Aggie was so serious. Perhaps someone as lighthearted and cheerful as Karen seemed to be would serve to draw her out of her shell. Leslie began to feel better about this idea after all. ''And, about the financing,'' she said, still a little wary about that aspect of things.

''No need to worry about that,'' Karen said firmly. ''I'm being paid by the agency, and if they're happy with the grant money, then I don't see why you should have to worry about it.'' She smiled reassuringly. ''The agency was founded by a rich widow who felt that all young people need a secure base in life through education. That's why we're willing to take on people like Aggie. Because there is a need to be met.''

At that moment, Joe returned with Aggie. As usual, she looked distracted, as if her mind were on some other planet. And as if she had no intention of returning to this one. ''Aggie,'' Joe said, ''this is Karen.''

Karen held out her hand and gave one of her wide smiles that would have melted a snowman. ''Hi. Nice to meet you.''

Aggie ignored her hand, and didn't even look up at Karen. Leslie frowned at this rudeness, but Karen seemed to take it in her stride.

''Aggie's such a pretty name,'' she continued, using her hand to smooth her skirt slightly, as if that was really what she'd intended all along. ''Is it short for anything? Agatha?''

At that, Aggie looked up, a faint frown on her face. But she still didn't say anything.

Karen laughed. ''Agoraphobia?'' she guessed. That got her an increase in the frown, but also a certain amount of attention from Aggie. Continuing as if this were perfectly normal—and maybe for her it *was*—Karen said, "Hey, I've got an idea. Want to show me your room?"

Leslie looked nervously at Joe. Was that a wise idea? Aggie might throw one of her temper tantrums if a stranger invaded her space. On the other hand, if Karen were going to work here, then she and Aggie would have to come to some kind of terms.

Joe nodded at his daughter. "Go on," he said. "Show her."

Wordlessly, Aggie spun around and marched toward the stairs. Flicking Leslie a reassuring smile, Karen followed her. Joe glanced down at Leslie, and must have seen the tension in her face.

"Don't worry," he murmured. "This is going to work out great. If anyone can get through to Aggie, I think Karen will. She has a real knack for this sort of thing."

"Maybe," Leslie agreed hesitantly. "But what if no one *can* get through to Aggie? What then?"

Joe put an arm around her shoulder. "I think we've got enough problems without trying to invent any more, honey. Let's just take it as it comes and see what happens, shall we? So far, it looks good."

Nodding, Leslie tried to bury all her worries and doubts. It was going to take time, she knew. And worrying wouldn't help at all. But it was something that was very difficult to stop.

Aggie led the way into her room, and eyed the strange woman through half-closed lids.

Karen Ross looked around the room, grinning widely. "This is a lovely room," she commented. "What a nice bed."

Aggie thought it was kind of young for her, all pinks and

pastels, but she didn't see any reason to share this information with the woman.

Then Karen's eyes lit on Aggie's collection of stuffed animals and puppets. "Hey, they're terrific. You want to know a secret?"

Aggie looked at her without interest. She didn't care whether Karen spoke or not. She didn't care if Karen stayed or not. She didn't care if Karen tried to teach her or not. It made no difference to her. Nobody had asked her if *she* wanted a tutor. But nobody asked her very much at all. And if they did, they didn't believe anything she told them.

Karen refused to be put off. In a conspiratorial whisper, she confided to Aggie, "I have a collection of stuffed toys in my room at home, too. I love them. Can I take a look at yours?"

Aggie shrugged. She didn't care. As Karen started to peer at them all, Aggie tried to ignore her. Then the Voice was back in her head. *Watch this one; she's tricky. I can't tell what she's thinking.* Aggie smirked to herself. *I don't care what she's thinking,* she told the Voice. *I don't care about anything to do with her.*

With a cry of delight, Karen snatched up a puppet koala bear. "This is delightful," she said. "I've always had a thing for koalas. They're just so cute."

Aggie felt like throwing up. How nauseating! It was getting harder and harder to ignore this person, though, no matter how hard she tried. And there was something . . . not quite right about her. Aggie couldn't fathom it.

Karen slipped her hand into the puppet, and then went to sit on the bed. She made it dance a few steps, and then grinned up at Aggie. "Can you make her dance like this?"

"Yes," Aggie said, bored stupid by this woman. She'd forgotten that she was trying to ignore her. "It's no big deal."

Karen considered this for a second, and then nodded.

"You're right. It's no big deal." She pulled her hand out of the puppet.

Aggie went white.

The koala was still dancing, with no hand inside of it. . . .

Suddenly terrified, Aggie whirled and ran away from the room and its disturbing occupant. She heard Karen call, "Aggie!", but she didn't stop. She ran into the bathroom and locked the door. Then she hunkered down in the far corner, trying to burrow into the back wall for protection.

What kind of person was Karen?

Nobody could make a puppet dance on its own like that! It was impossible, and scary. Aggie felt the fear welling up inside of her. For a second she was afraid that things were going to start to break again, and that she'd get into more trouble. Then she realized that it wasn't that kind of feeling. It wasn't anger, which *did* things around her; this was straight, simple fear.

What is Karen?

There was a gentle tap on the door. "Aggie." It was Karen's voice, gentle and pleading. "Open the door, please."

You've got to be joking! Aggie thought. She wanted nothing at all to do with this horrifying person. Whatever she'd done to the puppet . . . Aggie shook her head. She wouldn't come out while Karen was still in the house.

Then she saw the bolt on the door. It wobbled slightly, and then started to draw back. Nobody was touching it. It was just like the puppet, coming to life on its own. It had to be Karen doing this, somehow. Aggie whimpered in fear, and hugged her knees to her, compressing herself into as small a shape as possible. *Go away!* she wanted to scream, but she couldn't. She was much too scared to speak.

The door opened, and Karen came in. She was holding the koala puppet in one hand. The other was at her throat. From the blouse, she had pulled a thin crystal on a golden chain, and she was holding it out from her neck. The crystal seemed to be almost glowing with light.

"Go away," Aggie begged, terrified.

"Did I scare you, Aggie?" Karen asked gently. She halted about five feet from her, and then crouched down.

"Go away!" insisted Aggie, breathing fast and shallow. Her heart was pounding away, and she could hear the thrumming of her pulse in her ears.

"If I scared you, I'm sorry," Karen said in a soft, calming voice. "I didn't mean to. I only meant to show you what I can do."

"What you can do?" repeated Aggie. Her eyes fixed on the puppet, now lifeless in Karen's hand. "Why? What are you? Mary Poppins from hell?"

Karen laughed, genuinely amused. "Hardly." Her lips twitched. "But I think you know why I showed you what I can do, Aggie."

"No," Aggie said defiantly. "I don't know."

Karen held out the lifeless puppet, and Aggie snatched it from her hand. She clutched it to her chest, feeling somehow slightly protected from this stranger.

"Because," Karen said, "you're just like me, Aggie. You can do the same things."

Aggie refused to hear this. "No, I can't!" she growled. "I'm not like anybody." This person couldn't possibly know what she was like, what she was going through. What it was like to be her.

"Yes, you are, Aggie," Karen insisted, still in that soft, gentle voice of hers. "People don't understand you. They don't believe you. They don't know you're not like them. And you can't understand *why* you're not just the same as they are. Things happen on their own when you're around, don't they? Things break, or fly, or just *happen*. And people don't like you because of it. And they don't believe you when you say you've done nothing.''

Aggie stared at the woman in confusion. She was describing some of the things that were really bothering Aggie. But how could she? Was it possible that somebody might actually *listen* to her and believe her? No. She couldn't take that chance. She'd been hurt too much already by rejection. Karen might claim to be on her side right now, but it wouldn't last. It couldn't.

''I don't make things happen,'' Aggie said defiantly. ''They just *do*.'' Her fear was ebbing a bit, and it was being replaced by resentment.

''Yes, you do,'' Karen insisted. ''You simply don't know *how* you're doing it. But I can teach you to control that power, Aggie. All you have to do is give me a chance.''

She *didn't* understand at all, just as Aggie had suspected. ''I don't want to *control* it!'' she yelled angrily. ''I want it to go away!'' The anger overcame her fear, and she pushed to her feet, dodged past Karen and then ran down the stairs, panting hard. She dashed into the living room, where her parents were waiting, and then threw herself into a chair, clutching the puppet to herself as if she were a child again.

She didn't know what to think. Her mind was a whirl of questions with no answers. Primary among them was: *What is Karen?*

The young woman entered the room as if nothing was wrong, wearing another of her stupid smiles. She smiled too much; Aggie couldn't trust anybody who smiled so much. *Nobody* could be that happy. She had to be faking it.

Aggie glanced up at her folks, who were holding one another, worried expressions on their faces. *They're scared that you've put Karen off,* the Voice told her. *They're getting ready to blame you for ruining their last chance.*

Their last chance? Aggie was getting mad again. What

about *her* life? Nobody seemed to be bothered about that. They all wanted to just control her, make her do what they felt was right. But they simply didn't understand her. None of them. *Especially* not Karen, if she thought that Aggie wanted to stay like this the rest of her life.

Maybe she was right, and there was something inside of her that somehow did make things happen. Aggie didn't really believe it, but it was possible. If that was true, she wanted it out, gone and buried, so that she could go back to being normal once again. That was all she wanted out of her life—a chance to be *normal* once more.

Her mother stared at Aggie in concern. "Is everything all right, honey?" she asked.

She means "What have you done now?" the Voice said helpfully. Aggie ignored them both.

"Everything's fine," Karen said easily. "I think Aggie and I will get along just great. We're already warming up to one another."

Liar! thought Aggie. But she didn't say anything.

Her father looked from her to Karen and back again. He plastered a fake smile on his face. "What do you think, Aggie?" he asked her. "Would you like to have Karen come to tutor you?" But Aggie knew he *really* meant "Don't drive her out! She's our last chance!"

Their last chance, not hers.

"Honey?" her mother asked. "It's up to you. Do you want Karen to stay?"

Up to me? Aggie almost felt like laughing at that. They *wanted* her to say yes. She could feel it so strongly that if she had a knife she could have cut it and spread it on bread for lunch. Who were they trying to fool? If she said *no*, then what? Would they really say to Karen, "Thanks, but get lost?"

No way.

Aggie stared at Karen, who smiled back.

What is she? Aggie didn't know. Unlike other people, the Voice didn't seem able to connect with Karen. Not even a vague idea what she was really thinking. *She's dangerous,* the Voice told her. *Be very careful with her.*

Would she go away if Aggie insisted? Aggie didn't really think so. She had a determined look about her. And she seemed to be convinced that she could help Aggie. She *did* know something of what Aggie was going through. Maybe, just maybe, she could talk to Karen about what really hurt. . . . Or was she just being a fool to even consider it?

She looked from one adult to the others. In her parents' faces that one message: Don't mess up! Say yes! In Karen's face . . . what?

"I guess," she finally managed to bring herself to say. It was probably best to have Karen where she could keep an eye on the weird woman.

Her father gave a great sigh of relief. The right answer! "Well, then," he said to Karen. "I guess that means you have a job."

"Excellent." Karen gave the whole room a wide grin. "I'm looking forward to it. If it's okay with you, I'll start tomorrow." She reached for her backpack. "In the meantime, I'd better find somewhere to stay."

Leslie nudged Joe, and Aggie had a sudden sinking feeling. They'd obviously been talking about things while Aggie and Karen were gone, and Aggie had a dreadful certainty that she knew what it was.

"Well, actually," Joe said nervously, "we've got a spare room, and since your agency is picking up your fees, well, we thought that the least we could do was to offer you a place to stay."

Another powerful smile. "That is so kind of you," Karen said. "Thank you so much. It would make things a great deal easier, wouldn't it?'' She smiled at Aggie. ''It looks like we're going to be next-door neighbors, too.''

Aggie's heart felt as if it had slammed into the floor. *Terrific*. Now there would be no escaping her at all. . . .

What new nightmare was this that she'd been thrown into?

CHAPTER 5

Mrs. Hagen didn't think that her life could possibly have gotten any worse. She was only just starting to realize how wrong she could be. It had been just twenty-two days since she had last seen her daughter. Twenty-two days of sheer hell. Twenty-two mornings of waking up and wondering if there was something—*anything*—she should or could have done so that Lucy would be here, now, with her. Instead of . . . wherever she was.

Twenty-two days of fear, pain, and uncertainty. Of the police telling her that they still didn't have a clue as to where her daughter might be. Mrs. Hagen didn't like to think of it, but she was so terrified that Lucy was with some human monster who wanted her for his own unspeakable ends.

And now this. Another policeman, wanting them to go over and over the same grounds they'd trod fruitlessly before. He had an ID card that said he was from some federal investigation bureau.

He was a man you could sum up in a single word: crumpled. His suit looked as though he slept in it, which he might. His tie was slightly crooked and rumpled. His face was lined, and his thin, gray hair was untamable. He looked tired and cynical, as if he'd rather be anywhere else now than here with her and her husband. He looked up from the photo of Lucy that she had handed him, and slipped the photo into his pocket.

''And how long has she been missing, Mr. Hagen?'' he asked. His voice sounded worn, too, as if it was tired out from overuse. His eyes, she noticed, were bloodshot. Like her own. Insomnia did that to you. But how could she sleep, knowing that Lucy was most likely in danger. If she was even still al—

Stop that! Lucy *was* alive! She couldn't stop believing that for a second!

''Three weeks,'' her husband replied tiredly. ''Look, we've already been through all of this with the police, several times. I would think you people would have better things to do than question us over and over again.''

Walsh moved his head sideways just a couple of inches. ''Our agency likes to conduct its own investigation.''

''I see.'' Mr. Hagen was tense, naturally, and not about to be intimidated. ''And what agency was that again? The FBI?''

''No, sir.'' Walsh gave a thin smile. ''My agency has a slightly narrower focus than the FBI. We concentrate on missing children, like Lucy. It's all we do, and that means we're pretty good at it.'' He pulled a notebook from his pocket. The edges were bent back, and it looked as worn as he did. He fished a ballpoint from an inside pocket and flicked through the pages to the one he wanted. ''To be honest, the police have very little chance of recovering your daughter. Oh, I know they'll do their best, but they don't have the resources or leads that my department has. Believe me, cooperating with us is your best way of getting Lucy back.''

Mr. Hagen nodded. "All right," he agreed. "Anything you want. Anything that might help Lucy."

"Good." Walsh studied his page and then looked at Mrs. Walsh. "When was she last seen?"

Mrs. Hagen knew the answer to that, as she knew the answer to everything else about that day. Except the one most important question. "She was walking home from school. It's only eight blocks. People saw her leave the playground and walk toward a bus stop. And then . . . then she was just gone." There was a catch in her throat, and Walsh gave her a sympathetic smile.

"There's no rush, Mrs. Hagen," he said. "I know that this must be painful for you. What did her friends say?"

"Well . . ." She wondered how honest she ought to be about this. Then she realized that withholding anything from him might endanger the chances of getting Lucy back. "She didn't have many friends. Lucy could be . . . difficult . . . at times. The other students saw her leave alone, and didn't pay any more attention to her."

"I see." Walsh didn't sound surprised at the news. "Is there any chance that she'd have accepted a ride home?"

"No, never," Mrs. Hagen protested. "Not from anyone she didn't know. We always drummed it into her how foolish and dangerous that could be. And Lucy has too much common sense to do anything stupid like that." *Anyone she didn't know* . . . That was the nightmare. What if whoever had taken her was someone she knew? One of the policemen had mentioned that in kidnap cases like this, most were by people known to the victim. Mrs. Hagen had spent hours thinking of all the people Lucy might have accepted a ride from—friends, family, neighbors. And then she had tried picturing each and every one of them as possibly having abducted Lucy. It made looking at any one of those people painful, and staying in a room with them almost unendurable.

"Is it possible that she was picked up by your nanny?" asked Walsh. He consulted his notes. "Martha?"

"Martha?" Mrs. Walsh blinked, astonished. That was one person she'd never had a suspicion about. "Martha wasn't even in town. A week before Lucy . . . disappeared, Martha had an emergency call from a family member in Florida. She handed in her resignation and left. She was distraught at leaving Lucy, but had no choice. We were in the process of interviewing replacements for her when Lucy . . ." Her voice trailed off as she fought back tears.

Her husband scowled. "You don't think Martha had something to do with this, do you?"

"Oh, God," muttered Mrs. Walsh. Lucy had loved Martha; so had she and her husband. She'd been so good for Lucy, coaxing her out of her shell and cheering her up once again. That she could have betrayed this obvious affection seemed almost unthinkable.

Almost.

Walsh didn't answer directly. Instead, he fished inside his pocket and pulled out a photo, which he offered to Mrs. Hagen. "Is this a photo of Martha?"

She didn't need to study it very long. It had been taken through a telephoto lens and was a little grainy and blurred, but there was no mistaking that wide smile, the long, blondish hair, and the long skirt and boots. "Yes," she said softly. Then she couldn't stop the tears anymore. They started trickling down her cheeks. Her husband handed her a tissue, and she dabbed at her eyes. "She couldn't have had anything to do with . . ." she began. Then she hiccupped and tried again. "She loved Lucy."

Walsh took back the photo and slipped it back into his pocket. "Tell me what you know about *Martha*," he said, stressing the name slightly.

"She . . . she was new in town, so she didn't have many

friends,'' Mrs. Hagen explained. ''She did mention that she was an only child, so maybe that was part of it. Why she kept to herself so much, I mean. She spent most of her time with Lucy. They adored one another.''

Impatiently, Walsh shook his head. ''No, I mean *details*. Did she give you a forwarding address for her mail, for example? A social security number? Phone numbers? Did she have her own phone, call people?''

Mr. Hagen shook his head. ''My wife told you, she kept to herself. She never called anyone. There were two, maybe three calls for her while she lived here. They were from another woman. An aunt, Martha told us. That was it. We didn't have a social security number, no.'' He looked embarrassed.

''Off the books,'' Walsh grunted. ''Yes, I figured that out. It was a long shot. How about a forwarding address?''

''No.'' Mrs. Walsh shook her head. ''She didn't get very much mail at all. She was here for two months, and in that time she had only one letter and perhaps three packages. I don't know if they were from home. I bring in the mail every day, and I couldn't help noticing . . .''

That seemed to spark some interest in Walsh's tired eyes. ''Do you still have any of those packages?'' he asked eagerly.

''I'll go and look,'' Mr. Hagen said. He left the room.

There was a silence, and Mrs. Hagen felt compelled to speak. ''They were like sisters, you must understand. Lucy and Martha were always together. Martha would never have harmed her. I'm sure of that.''

''I didn't say she had *harmed* her, Mrs. Hagen,'' Walsh answered slowly. ''And I've not even stated that she was involved in your daughter's disappearance. But there are other reasons to take a child other than to harm them. Which doesn't mean they're any less sick.'' He thought for a moment. ''Did Martha ever give Lucy anything? A gift?''

"Yes." Mrs. Hagen smiled sadly. "She was always buying things for Lucy."

"I'm thinking of something specific," Walsh explained. "A small crystal on a chain, maybe?"

Amazed, Mrs. Hagen nodded. "Yes, she gave Lucy the prettiest little crystal. How ever did you know about that?"

Walsh didn't get a chance to reply. Her husband returned, his hands empty.

"I guess we must have thrown the last package out," he apologized. "And Martha took whatever came in them with her when she left. There's nothing in her old room."

The hope seemed to have fled from Walsh's eyes at this news. Mrs. Hagen felt a pang of pain, and realized that the packages might—just might—be a clue to Lucy's whereabouts. She concentrated hard.

"I do recall something about them," she said, and hope flared in Walsh's face again. "They all had one of those pretty little return address labels on them. This was of a row of books. It said Antiquarian . . . no, wait a minute: Antiquarius Books. I remember thinking it sounded rather New Age, like Aquarius."

Walsh nodded eagerly, writing this down in his tattered notebook. "And the city?"

Downhearted, she admitted: "I only remember the name of the store. I didn't want to pry, you understand. I only noticed the name because of the label. I hope it helps."

"It's a start," Walsh answered gratefully. He stood up. "Thanks very much." He started to turn and head for the door.

Mrs. Hagen grabbed his arm. "Do you think you're going to find Lucy?" she demanded.

Walsh considered the question for a moment, and then tried a smile. It wasn't too convincing. "We'll do our best," he promised. "We don't have much to go on, but we have something. I'll be in touch again soon, so if you remember anything else at all about Martha, no matter how insignificant it is, keep it in mind. Anything at all might help us to find her."

"And Lucy?" persisted Mrs. Hagen.

"If it's not too late," was as much as he would promise. Gently, he pulled free of her grip. "I promise, I'll keep you informed." Then he turned and left.

Mrs. Hagen looked at her husband. He came to her and held her in a tight embrace. "It's a possibility," he murmured. "We have to have faith."

Yes. She had to have faith. She had to hope.

And that was the worst hell of all.

Walsh reached his car and slid into the driver's seat. The interior was as crumpled as he was, and littered with fast-food bags and empty coffee cups. He pushed this morning's cup aside, and fished out his cellular phone. He speed-dialed the office, and said immediately, "This is Walsh. Patch me to Selma."

A moment later, Selma came on the line. She was one of the best computer operatives in Washington, and one of his most valuable resources. "Yeah, Selma," he said. "I think I may have a lead." He consulted his notebook. "I need a location on an Antiquarius Bookstore somewhere in the continental U.S. I have no idea of the town or state. When you find it"—he wasn't going to say *if*—"then I'll need tickets from here to wherever it is. And a rental car waiting for me."

"And if there's more than one?" she asked.

"I don't care how many of them there are," he growled. "I'll check them all out if I have to. I have to find her." Then he replaced the phone, and started the car. He could feel sorry for the Hagens. Losing an only child like this had to be one of the worst things in the world.

He didn't have the heart to tell them that there was absolutely no chance that they would ever see their little girl again.

CHAPTER 6

THINGS HAD QUIETED down in the bookstore, and Ruth was filling in gaps among the books when the phone on her desk rang. She hurried to answer it. "Antiquarius Books."

"Hi, it's Karen. Can I speak to Jean?"

Ruth called across the store to the older woman, "It's Karen." She was well used to referring to their operatives by their aliases. It would be a grave mistake to slip and call them by their *real* names. That way, they might be traced.

Going to her desk, Jean picked up her own line. "Karen?"

"Yes," came the reply. "I'm in a phone booth. I just wanted you to know that I've made contact. We definitely have a positive."

"Excellent," Jean answered. "How long will it be before she's ready?"

"I don't know yet," Karen said. "She's very withdrawn. It may take a while before I can get her to trust me. But she seems to be particularly powerful. I wouldn't want to make a mistake and allow her to escape. There is one other thing. Her mother seemed to be a little suspicious that I was too young to be a tutor. She'll likely call to confirm.''

''Not a problem,'' Jean said briskly. ''Stay with it. I'll cover your background. If the Travis girl is as powerful as you think, I want her very badly. Use your judgment, Karen. You'll know when the best time comes to take her.''

Aggie wasn't sure what to make of Karen. In some ways, the young tutor was very pleasant. She was obviously trying to be, and she had a terrific smile. On the other hand, she was also very secretive. Oh, she talked all the time about her family and things like that, but Aggie couldn't see anything past the surface. No matter how hard she tried, she couldn't make Karen out. It was like trying to see through a brick wall.

And she was convinced there was something not quite right about her. The problem was that Aggie couldn't figure out what it was. Normally if someone lied to her, the Voice could tell. It would whisper the truth to Aggie's mind. But the Voice was completely silent about Karen. It couldn't read her at all, and that bothered Aggie.

What bothered her even more was that she realized she'd become dependent on the Voice. It was one of the things that set her apart from normal people, she knew. She'd always believed that she wanted nothing more than to get rid of it. Now, when it wasn't working right, she was frustrated and angry with it.

There was a tap on her door, and Karen entered, carrying a glass of soda and a straw. ''I thought you might be thirsty,'' she said cheerily, placing the glass down on the bedside table. Without being invited, she sat on the bed next to Aggie. ''And that maybe we could get to know one another a bit better.''

Aggie stared coldly back at her. "You're my tutor," she said. "That's all I need to know about you."

Karen shook her head. "No, we need to know a lot more about each other, Aggie. I can't teach you if I don't know what you like, and what interests you. What do you like doing with your friends?"

Aggie snorted. That showed how much Karen knew. "Nobody wants to be friends with me," she replied. "They all think I'm a freak."

"Do *you* think you're a freak?" Karen asked, suddenly serious.

Aggie considered the point. "I must be," she said. "I know I'm not like everyone else."

"That's not really true," Karen countered. "True, you're not like *everyone* else. But you're not the only one like you. There are others who are very much like you."

Aggie shrugged. "If there are, I don't know any. And they probably wouldn't want to be my friends anyway."

Leaning forward, Karen said, "I want to be your friend."

Right! Aggie grunted. "You're paid to do that, so it doesn't count."

"No," Karen answered. "I'm paid to be your tutor. I *choose* to be your friend. That's different, isn't it?"

Aggie considered the point for a moment. There was something to what the young woman was saying. Maybe she was just being too suspicious, and Karen really did just want to be her friend. Or maybe this was some kind of trick to motivate her to learn. Aggie had always been disappointed by people she'd thought might be her friends. Why would Karen be any different? "I guess," she finally said, committing herself to nothing.

Karen nodded, and then changed the subject slightly. "I used to get those headaches, too."

Scowling, Aggie asked her, "What headaches?"

"The ones that you get whenever you get mad," Karen answered. "When the rage builds up inside you and things happen. I used to get them, too."

"You did?" Aggie studied her curiously. Was she telling the truth? Or was this just an attempt to gain her confidence?

"Yes." Karen thought for a moment. "And I could sometimes see this glow of light around people. All different colors, and if I tried real hard, squeezed down tight, I could make things happen to those people, especially if they'd made me mad."

Aggie realized with a shock that Karen was describing what was happening to her. She'd not told Karen anything about the lights, or about using the glow to get her own back. How could Karen know unless . . . ?

The young woman nodded. "You're not alone, Aggie. There are others like you. Including me."

If that was true . . . then maybe she wasn't really a freak! Maybe this was normal for some people. Aggie *wanted* desperately to believe Karen. But she was also afraid to believe her. What if Karen was lying for some reason? She didn't want to be let down again. It *sounded* like Karen knew what she was going through, and it would be wonderful to be able to trust her and have someone to share her feelings and problems with. On the other hand, she'd expected her parents to believe in her and trust her—and they just thought she was a destructive liar. Maybe Karen was just pretending to be her friend.

Karen must have seen the hope and confusion on her face. She smiled gently, and reached over to the glass of soda. "Watch the straw," she said. She rested her finger on the top of it, and then moved the straw into the center of the glass, so that it stood upright. "If I take my finger away, the straw will fall back, right?"

"Right," agreed Aggie.

Karen nodded, and took her finger away.

The straw didn't move.

Eyes wide, Aggie stared at the straw, and then at Karen, who now had a slight smile on her face. She was being spooky again, like she had been with the puppet. But this time it seemed a little less shocking. Maybe Aggie was getting used to it. She frowned at the straw, which still refused to fall. "How did you do that?" she finally asked.

"I focused," Karen answered. She let the straw fall back. "You can see a halo of light around people and things, can't you, Aggie?"

Aggie nodded.

"Well, I can see it, too. And that's just the first step. When the anger overcomes you, it's like a stream of light flows from you to whatever's around you, isn't it?"

Again, Aggie nodded. It sounded as if Karen *did* know something about her problem.

"Well," Karen explained, "when you're angry, the light just lashes out. That's why it breaks things, you see. It's uncoordinated and unfocused. What you have to do is concentrate, get that light down to a point, and then make it do what *you* want it to do."

It sounded simple, but Aggie knew it couldn't be. "It gets all goofed up when I do it," she objected. "I can't control it. It just *happens*."

"No," Karen said firmly. "That's because you don't know any better. You don't know how to control it yet. But it doesn't have to go wrong. You have to control it, and not allow it to control you." She reached into a pocket in her skirt and drew out something that caught Aggie's attention. It was a thin crystal, pale, with a hint of blueness, on a gold chain. Karen held it out. "Here, this is for you. It will help you to focus. Go on, take it."

Aggie eyed it suspiciously. She wasn't sure she wanted to

accept anything yet from Karen. And, even more to the point, she couldn't see how a lump of crystal could help at all.

Karen reached into the top of her blouse, and pulled out the crystal that hung on a chain around her neck. "I have one, too," she explained. "I don't need it as often now, but at the beginning, I was like you. I couldn't control my abilities. I really needed this." She held out the crystal in her palm again. "Just try it, okay?"

Aggie shrugged, and took the jewel. A little self-consciously, she hung it around her neck. She held the tip of the crystal in her left hand, as Karen was doing.

"That's it," Karen said gently. "Now, just look at the straw again, but keep the crystal just in view. Try to reach out with your thoughts. Visualize the light in your aura reaching out to the straw and just very gently nudging it into place. Go on."

Aggie tried. She stared at the straw, and half squinted at the crystal. *Move!* she willed it, trying to make it stand straight. But nothing seemed to happen, and she shook her head in despair. "I can't do it!" she snapped. Maybe Karen was wrong about her, and she *couldn't* control her light.

But Karen refused to let her give up. "Yes, you can," she said firmly. "Don't get mad. That will just make things get out of control, and you'll get *both* of us into trouble this time. Just concentrate, very gently but firmly, on the straw, and keep your anger out of it. Don't feel frustrated, just feel relaxed and focused."

Aggie tried again, concentrating on the straw, and on the crystal. It did seem to have some sort of soothing effect on her mind. Her anger started to fade away. Karen reached out and used the tip of her finger to stand the straw up straight.

"Concentrate," she murmured. "Focus on keeping the straw upright as I take away my finger. . . ." She slowly took it away from the straw.

And the straw didn't fall.

Aggie knew that somehow she was doing it. She had managed to make the straw stand up, just through the power of her mind! It was kind of exciting and scary at the same time. It was also tiring. She could feel her face turning red as she concentrated on the straw.

It started to wobble, and she tried to correct it. She pictured it standing up straight and alert again in her mind, and focused through the crystal she clutched in her left fist. The straw shook, and then flew like a rocket from the glass and across the room, where it slid to the floor. The glass shook so hard that it rattled.

"I can't do it!" Aggie snapped in frustration.

Karen picked up the straw and replaced it in the glass. "You *can* do it," she insisted. "You were doing it. You were very close. Just try it again, Aggie. Focus only on the straw. Block out all of your other thoughts and fears. Just the straw matters." She slowly took her finger away.

And the straw stayed in place.

Aggie frowned as she focused, and then another thought came to her. "You're doing it," she accused Karen. "You're trying to make me think it's me, but it's really you doing that."

"No," Karen said, shaking her head. "You're doing it, all by yourself. And you're doing it very well."

Was she? Was Karen telling the truth? Or was she really doing it herself, and just wanted Aggie to *think* she was doing it? Well, there was one way to find out the truth. She just had to do something different to the straw, something that Karen wouldn't know about. She changed her thought from *Stand up straight* to *Fly!*

The straw immediately took off like a rocket, and slammed into the ceiling before falling back to the carpet.

"It *was* me," Aggie said, a little breathlessly. She stared at the straw and then the crystal in astonishment. ''I *controlled* it.''

Karen abruptly gave her a hug. ''Yes,'' she agreed when she let Aggie go. ''You were controlling it. That's the first step to take.''

Aggie didn't know what to make of it all. For the first time, instead of striking out in anger and breaking things, she'd reached out gently and affected something. Instead of being ashamed and disgusted by herself, Aggie now started to feel hopeful. ''Did you hurt people when you got mad?'' she asked.

''Yes,'' Karen replied. ''Until I learned how to control it. Then I could stop doing things to people.''

Aggie frowned. ''I don't know if I want to stop hurting people,'' she said honestly. ''I never start it. It's always after they do something to me. Then they *deserve* to get hurt.''

''I know.'' Karen gave her a firm look. ''But it's not right, Aggie. It's wrong to use our special abilities to hurt other people.''

''Why?'' Aggie demanded. ''If they start it, why shouldn't I hurt them back?''

''Because it isn't right,'' Karen explained. ''Look, people like us with these powers have been given a tremendous gift—and also a great responsibility. Other people can't do what we can do. To use our powers to hurt them would be the worst form of bullying. We have to learn to use our powers for good ends, not evil ones. Besides, once you learn to focus, you'll stop feeling so angry and frustrated. Then things won't happen around you, and people will stop being scared of you. Then they won't be so mean to you, and you won't need to strike back at them. It'll all work out.'' She gave Aggie a big smile. ''It'll all work out, I promise. We'll practice together, every day. Just the two of us. You'll be amazed how easy it will seem to control your powers soon.''

Aggie finally felt hope. Karen *did* seem to know what she was talking about. And the crystal she had given Aggie helped her to focus her thoughts. To be rid of all that anger! To stop breaking things! If that happened, then Mom and Dad would start to love her again, instead of thinking she was a destructive little liar. Things would get better! Excitedly, Aggie suddenly couldn't wait to try again. She focused her mind through the crystal and stared at the books on her desk.

Instead of standing there in line, she made them pop in and out like dancers. One two, one two, one two . . . She laughed delightedly as she watched the books move.

"Well," Karen said dryly, "it looks like you aren't going to need a whole lot of practice, young lady."

Maybe not. But Aggie had a suspicion that she was going to have some fun at last finding out.

CHAPTER 7

WALSH STOOD OUTSIDE the bookstore, looking up at the slightly worn sign over the door: ANTIQUARIUS BOOKS. The window was decked out with a display of New Age books on topics ranging from reading Tarot cards to white witchcraft. A slight smile lit his own worn face. He remembered his youth, far too long ago. There had been a store like this that he'd spent hours inside, buying books for a nickel or a dime on any subject you could imagine back then. He'd explored strange alien worlds, treasure-hunted lost Troy, and ventured up the Amazon. . . .

He shrugged off those old, fond memories. There would be nothing like them inside this shop. The cheapest book here would be priced in dollars, maybe even in double-digit dollars. And some of the rarer books would cost hundreds and even thousands of dollars. A long way from that slightly musty old shop of his youth.

Pushing open the door, Walsh stepped inside. He was immediately greeted by that old, familiar book smell, as fusty as ever. Well, maybe some things never changed. A shame *he* had changed so much since then, and this wasn't a pleasure stop, but business. And business of the dirtiest kind. Just inside the door was a bookcase filled with paperbacks. A sign saying 50 CENTS EACH made him smile ruefully. It was almost like going back home again.

Except the owners of the store where he used to go didn't kidnap children.

Walsh scanned the store. There were a couple of customers browsing the shelves, and two women behind two different desks. One, behind the checkout, was young. Probably mid-twenties, with a pleasant face and a small name tag telling the world her name was Ruth. The other, older one, sat at a desk further back, going through some papers beside a computer. Walsh moved across to Ruth.

See if he could get a response . . . "Excuse me," he asked politely, "do you have any books on the human genome program?"

"Genome program?" Ruth asked, a slightly puzzled expression on her face. "I'm sorry, I'm not entirely sure what that would be. Is it something to do with medicine?"

"Genetics," Walsh clarified. "Inherited traits, that kind of thing." Either she didn't know what he was talking about, or else she was a very good actress.

"I'll check," she answered, bending to a list of recent arrivals, which she went down, using her finger to trace her path.

Walsh leaned forward slightly, watching as she perused the entries. He could see that she wore nothing around her neck. So she probably wasn't one of the people he was looking for. Maybe she was hired just to run the store. Or maybe this wasn't the right place after all. Walsh hoped that wasn't the case. The name of the store had been the first break he'd gotten in years, and he sincerely hoped that it panned out and he'd struck gold. This had gone on for far longer than any of them had ever imagined when they had begun the project.

"No," Ruth said, looking up again. "We don't seem to have any books on the subject. But perhaps Jean can help you." She gave a smile. "She's a wizard at finding things I can't."

"Thank you," Walsh answered. He walked over to where the older woman was seated at her desk.

She seemed to sense him approaching. She closed the file folder she had been reading through and sat up straight. As she did so, Walsh caught the glint of gold and a sparkle of light reflected off a crystal around her neck.

Bingo! he thought happily. Of course, it was always possible that she was simply one of those people who believed in the helpful power of crystals, and it was tied to that display in the window. But Walsh refused to allow that possibility to exist. She simply *had* to be one of the people he was looking for.

"Can I help you?" she asked politely.

"I hope so," he replied. He leaned forward, apparently to read her name tag, but actually to get a better look at the crystal. It appeared to be identical to the one that the nanny Martha was wearing in the photograph he had. "Jean, is it?" He smiled at her, like a shark at its prey. "That's a very interesting crystal you're wearing. Where would I be able to get something like that?"

"It's one of a kind," she replied, slightly curtly.

Walsh grinned. "Oh, I'm sure I've seen something very like it before." He had absolutely no proof that she was connected to the kidnappings yet. There was no chance of a warrant to search this shop. But maybe he wouldn't need either if he played his cards right. It was just a matter of getting the enemy to make a mistake. Get them flustered, catch them off guard.

"Really?" Jean asked. He could hear the ice dripping from her voice. "Who are you?"

"Just a man with questions, Jean," he replied, going for the mock-friendly approach. "Someone who'd like to know how to get hold of one of those crystals. Or an eleven-year-old girl named Lucy Hagen. Or a nanny named Martha." He pulled the photo from his pocket and dropped it deliberately on the closed folder. "Funny how she's wearing one of your one-of-a-kind necklaces, too, isn't it? You don't happen to know her, do you?"

Jean was only human. She looked down at the photo. Walsh grinned again as he saw recognition dawn in Jean's eyes. And just a hint of fear. Walsh expected her to lie and say that she'd never seen the girl before, but he was pleasantly surprised by her response.

"She looks vaguely familiar. She might be a customer, I suppose."

Walsh had to admire that brazen attitude. "She might be," he agreed. "But I doubt it." He picked up the photo, and "accidentally" sent the file crashing to the floor. Newspaper clippings spilled out of it. "Oh, I'm so sorry. Let me help you—"

"Don't bother!" Jean snapped back, hastily gathering the clippings together and then placing the folder back on her desk with her elbow resting firmly on it. "I think you've done more than enough already."

"You may be right at that," Walsh agreed mildly. He could feel the inner turmoil that had to be raging through the woman.

From the direction of the checkout, Ruth called, "Jean? Is something wrong? Shall I call the police?"

Walsh turned an untroubled gaze onto Jean. "I wonder whose side they'd be on?" he asked softly.

She didn't answer him.

"Don't bother," Jean said. "He's just leaving." She gave him a dark look. "Aren't you?"

"I think so." He gave her a final smirk, and took a dog-eared business card from his wallet. It had only "Walsh" and his phone number on it. He dropped the card in front of her. "If you happen to remember who Martha is, or where Lucy Hagen can be found, give me a call anytime, night or day." He inclined his head slightly and then spun around. He gave Ruth a sweet smile on the way out, ignoring her frosty stare back, and then left the store.

There was a spring in his step. He had been right! That *was* the right bookstore! That woman, Jean, was definitely mixed up in the abductions. Of course, he could prove none of that. But he didn't have to. He'd walked in brazenly, told them he knew who they were and then left. If they didn't start panicking, then they weren't human. He was willing to bet anything that the two women in the store were even now up to something.

And when they moved, he'd be on their trail. He hadn't quite told them all the truth. The phone number on the business card would enable them to reach him anytime, that was true. Not that he expected them to call.

But the microtransmitter sandwiched inside the card would enable him to track them anywhere they might go. And he'd provoked Jean just enough to be certain that wherever she went, she'd take his card with her.

Maybe this was a really good day, after all.

Jean hastily shut down the computer, and then threw the file into her drawer and locked it. As she did so, Ruth came over to her, a worried frown on her face.

"What's wrong, Jean?" she asked.

"That man," Jean replied, picking up the business card. Just the one name and a phone number. No indication of whom he worked for. Not that she didn't already know, of course. There could only be one organization on her trail. . . . She slipped the card into her bag, and slung it over her shoulder. "I think we'd better start watching our tracks carefully," she said. "Run the shop as normal, and let everyone know that they may be followed."

"What are you going to do?" Ruth asked, frazzled.

"Just tell everyone that I'll be gone for a few days." Jean moved to the back room where her coat was. Time was of the essence right now. With Walsh on their trail . . .

Walsh sat in his car, humming happily to himself as he dialed the number he'd given Jean. "Selma? Walsh here. I've found *her*. She's got a new alias. Jean something. I just had a fun little face-to-face with her."

"Wonderful," Selma replied. "Shall I organize a raid?"

"No," Walsh answered. "I don't want her picked up quite yet."

"Why ever not?" Selma asked. "I'm sure we can get a warrant, even if you don't have much proof."

"Because," Walsh explained carefully, "she's no direct threat. She's over fifty. Her powers have to be minimal. But there's something going on. I'm certain they've selected another target. They won't want to stop partway through. I think Jean will lead me to their latest victim. I've rattled her cage pretty loudly. She may even lead me to their nest. So, for now, I want the shop placed under light surveillance, but absolutely no raids. We have to get them this time before they strike again, and I'm certain Jean's the key."

Selma thought for a moment before replying. "I'm sure you know what you're doing, Walsh," she agreed. "Very well.

We'll hold off from the store. Just don't lose the woman."

"Activate the card," he told her. "That way, we'll be able to track her wherever she goes."

"If she carries the card," Selma pointed out.

"She'll carry it," Walsh said with absolute confidence. "I've got her so worked up she'll carry it, even if it's just so she can curse me out. Ready the airport, just in case. I may need to get a ticket very quickly. I've a strong suspicion that they're going to move fast."

"You may be right," agreed Selma. "Still, I just hope that you haven't provoked them into doing anything hasty with their latest target."

Leslie was exhausted. All she wanted to do was to kick off her shoes, and sit back with a tall glass of iced tea. Work had been more frantic than usual today, and she'd agreed to a couple of hours' overtime. Thankfully, having Karen around was less expensive than she'd feared, but a few extra dollars didn't hurt. She let herself into the house and ran a hand through her hair. Catching a glimpse of herself in the hall mirror, she realized that her eyes looked really tired. *You're getting old,* she thought. *And you're nowhere near forty yet!* It was too depressing to contemplate. Instead, as she headed for the kitchen and the iced tea in the fridge, she called out, "Aggie! Aggie!"

There was no reply. In the past, this wouldn't have disturbed her too much. Aggie frequently went without talking for days on end. But since Karen had arrived, Aggie had started to loosen up. She seemed more cheerful, more relaxed. She had even started to smile again. And anyway, even if Aggie hadn't answered, Karen would have. She was supposed to be tutoring Aggie, after all.

The house was silent.

Suddenly worried, Leslie went into the study instead of the

kitchen. There were a couple of books open on the table, but nobody there.

"Aggie?" Leslie called again. "Karen?" There was a tightness in her chest, and a dull worry in her stomach. Despite her tiredness, she took the stairs two steps at a time as she rushed into Aggie's room.

There was nobody there. She was alone in the house.

Her daughter and the tutor had both vanished.

CHAPTER 8

LESLIE TRIED TO keep down her growing panic, but for a moment all she could think was: *My baby is missing!* Aggie was gone, and she didn't have any idea where or why. She started back downstairs, her mind a whirl of emotions and distraught thoughts. The phone, by the front door . . . Should she call Joe? The police? She had to do *something* to get her baby back!

And then the front door opened, and Karen walked in, followed by Aggie, who was just finishing an ice cream cone. Both seemed totally at ease, and oblivious to Leslie's state of near panic.

"Hi," Karen said casually.

The tension suddenly evaporated from Leslie's body, and she almost collapsed with relief. She'd been picturing all kinds of terrible disasters, and none of them were at all true. "I just got home," she said, her voice a little fast and shrill. "I didn't see anybody, and I was worried. You should have left a note."

Karen's brow furrowed. "I did." She pointed to the desk where Aggie's books were. There was a bright pink sticky note there. "I said we were going down to the park for a little exercise, and that we'd be back by"—she checked her watch—"about now, in fact." She seemed a little ill at ease. "Is that okay?"

Leslie snatched up the note, which did in fact say exactly what Karen claimed. Then she looked up, trying not to sound accusatory. "That's fine. I just didn't see the note, and I was worried. I'm sure you can understand that, can't you?"

"Of course," agreed Karen. "I'm sorry. Perhaps we'd better agree on where I should leave you notes in the future, so I don't cause you needless worry again."

That was a good idea, and Leslie nodded. Then she looked at Aggie, who had just finished her ice cream and was licking at her fingers. "Did you have fun?"

Aggie shrugged. "I guess."

"You guess?" Leslie shook her head. "Well, I suppose that's better than no."

Surprisingly, Aggie gave a tremulous smile. "I really like Karen," she volunteered.

Leslie's eyes widened. She'd not been expecting anything like that at all. Quite the opposite, if anything. Aggie had acted from the start as if Karen was an imposition she didn't want and that she'd resented. The first day had been a huge battle of wills, and Leslie was still amazed that there hadn't been any temper tantrums or anything broken since Karen had arrived. And now this! "Do you?" she asked. "Well, that's great. Go wash up, okay?"

"Sure." Instead of scowling, Aggie seemed almost happy as she ran upstairs to her bathroom.

Leslie shook her head in amazement and turned back to Karen. "Well, she certainly seems to like you," she commented. "You must have some kind of magic."

"I'm just trying to get through to her," Karen answered. "Aggie's a terrific kid, and once she gets done with growing, she'll be fine. This problem of hers is just an age thing that she'll grow out of. I'm just trying to help her see that."

"It's more than we've ever been able to do." Leslie couldn't keep a little resentment out of her voice. It was nice to see Aggie smiling again, true; but why couldn't it have been at her, instead of at Karen?

"I'm trained for this kind of thing," Karen said. "It's no reflection on you and Joe, or on what kind of parents you are. Aggie loves you, but she's just confused right now. I'm managing to convince her that I understand what she's going through, and so she relates to me because of it."

"Well, you certainly seem to be doing her good," Leslie had to confess. "I've not seen her this happy in a long time. Is she doing well with her studies?"

"Very well." Karen showed her the math book they'd been working on. Math was not one of Aggie's better subjects, but she certainly seemed to be doing fine. "Aggie's a very bright child. I know you must be proud of her. To be honest, her brightness is part of the problem. The other children probably resent her smartness, and that starts them picking on her. Aggie resents being different, and that's what started her problem. I'm trying to make her see that *different* doesn't mean *better* or *worse*, that it's just part of who she is. Once she can grasp that, I'm sure all of her problems will disappear."

Leslie nodded. It all sounded so wonderful. Karen was certainly getting through to Aggie.

So why did she still have this terrible feeling that all was not well?

Well, it was always possible to do something about it. Karen excused herself to go to her room, which was next to Aggie's. Once she was gone, Leslie moved to the filing cabinet. Inside were the papers that Karen had given them when she had arrived. Leslie found the agency's phone number and contact person, then went to the phone. She felt rather guilty, as if she were doing something underhanded, even though Karen had encouraged her to call. It was as if she were looking for some flaw in Karen. She felt as if there was some need to puncture her perfect exterior. After a moment's hesitation, she dialed the toll-free number.

Ruth looked up from the counter as the special phone on Jean's desk rang. With the older woman gone, she'd have to answer it. Jean had prepared her for this, but she couldn't help feeling a twinge of apprehension. She wasn't normally a very good liar. She was too open and honest for that. But now there was little option. Luckily, the store was empty. She'd have been incredibly embarrassed if anyone else had been present.

She picked up the phone, and managed an official-sounding voice. "Home Education Agency."

"Uh, hi," said the nervous voice on the other end. "This is Leslie Travis. One of your tutors is with us at the moment."

"Yes, Mrs. Travis?" Ruth replied, knowing she was blushing furiously but unable to control it. "I believe I know the case. I can pull the paperwork if that's necessary."

"Uh, no, not really," Mrs. Travis replied. She was definitely more nervous about this than Ruth was! "I just . . . well, it's Karen Ross . . ." Her voice trailed off.

Steeling herself, Ruth said crisply, "Is there a problem with Miss Ross? If so, she can be removed and a substitute will be allocated. Of course, you *would* have to file a report for us as to why Miss Ross is unsuitable." That should put her off!

"Oh, no, it's nothing like that," Mrs. Travis said hastily. "Quite the opposite, if anything. Aggie loves Karen, and there's not a problem."

"I see." Ruth was almost smiling now. This was a lot easier than she'd expected it to be. But Karen was good at her job. Of course she'd gained Aggie's confidence; her ability to get through to the most difficult children was why she was so invaluable. "Or, rather, I *don't* see, Mrs. Travis. If Miss Ross is working out fine, then why have you called about her?"

Ruth could almost feel the other woman squirming. "It's just that . . . well, she seems so *young* to be an experienced tutor."

"Oh, I see." Ruth poured as much sympathy and understanding into her voice as she could. "Well, Miss Ross did extremely well in our training program. She is, in fact, our second most highly trained tutor, despite her seeming youth. And we feel that her empathy with . . . troubled youngsters makes her even better in the field. I quite understand your concern, but please rest assured that we are constantly monitoring her progress."

There was a pause. Then: "Thank you. You make me feel a lot better about it."

"That's quite all right," Ruth answered. "And if there is any problem at all, please don't hesitate to call again, Mrs. Travis."

Ruth replaced the telephone feeling rather proud of herself. If only Jean had been here to hear how she'd handled it! Maybe she wasn't such a bad liar after all. . . .

That evening, Leslie could hear Karen and Aggie playing some computer game in the study. There was a great deal of laughter and some very odd noises from the computer. The door was shut, and Leslie couldn't help feeling excluded. Aggie was definitely doing better now than she had for months—but she was doing better for and with someone who was essentially a stranger.

Why couldn't you be like that with me, honey? she wondered. *Where did I go wrong? And how did Karen go so right?* It wasn't fair!

A pair of arms suddenly grabbed her and spun her around. Joe leaned forward and kissed her, a smile on his face. Leslie enjoyed the kiss for a moment, and then pretended to struggle free.

"Someone came home in a good mood," she commented, enjoying the feel of his arms enfolding her and his face close to hers.

"I'm happy," her husband replied. He nodded at the closed study door. "Listen to that. Aggie's happy. And because she's happy, I'm happy. I haven't seen her like this in a long time. It works."

"What works?" asked Leslie, frowning a little. She hadn't seen Joe this happy in a long time, either. The stress over Aggie had depressed them both far too much.

"Karen," Joe answered. Leslie couldn't help tensing slightly at this, and Joe was sensitive enough to her moods to pick up on it immediately. "What? Don't you like her?" He let her go, and led her through into the kitchen, away from where they might be overheard.

Trying to sort through all her own feelings, Leslie shook her head helplessly. "I like her," she admitted. "She's very easy to like. That smile, her genuine fondness for Aggie, the results she's getting . . ."

"But?" Joe prompted, knowing there was a lot Leslie wasn't saying.

"But she's too . . . perfect," Leslie complained. "A bit too good to be true."

Joe laughed. "Is that the problem? You're afraid that you're going to wake up and Karen was just a wonderful dream, and that things aren't going as well as they seem to be?"

It did sound childish the way he put it, but Leslie nodded stubbornly. ''Yes, something like that. I can't help feeling that there's a huge catch to all of this that we haven't seen yet. That there is going to be some terrible price to pay for Karen.''

''But we don't have to pay at all,'' Joe said, puzzled. ''Didn't you call her agency to check on that?''

''Yes,'' Leslie replied. ''But I'm not talking *money*, Joe. I mean some other sort of price.''

''I don't follow what you're saying,'' he admitted honestly.

''Well, you heard her laughing and playing with Karen,'' Leslie explained. ''And, earlier today, Aggie told me that she really likes Karen.''

''So what's the problem?''

Leslie sighed in exasperation. ''Joe, how long is it since Aggie laughed or played with *us*? Or told *us* that she really likes us?''

Joe grinned in relief. ''Oh, so *that's* the problem! You're afraid that Aggie is starting to like Karen better than she likes us, is that it? You're jealous of the relationship they've got.''

''No!'' Leslie exclaimed sharply. And then, more honestly and quietly: ''Well, yes. I suppose I am. Joe, I want that to be *me* in there with Aggie. I want to be the one she laughs with, the one she really likes. Not some stranger. I feel like Aggie may well be getting better, but that she's moving away from us as she does so. Like we're part of the problem that she's trying to cure.''

Joe took her hands in his and pulled her closer. ''I think you're just worrying about nothing, sweetheart. Karen's good for Aggie, and she's making her back into a little girl again, instead of that long streak of anger and misery she's had for months. As soon as she can, Aggie will begin opening up to us again. Until then, we have to be united and supportive. We have to let Aggie know that we're a hundred percent behind what Karen's doing." He searched her face carefully. "You *can* do that, can't you?"

"I suppose," Leslie agreed, with resignation. Joe didn't really understand her problem, and she didn't think she could explain it fully to him. She had carried Aggie for nine months, given birth to her daughter and raised her as best she could. It hurt terribly to see some other woman—younger, brighter, prettier—come into Aggie's life and then take what rightfully belonged to Leslie from her daughter. Of course it hurt. But if it was the best thing for Aggie, then she'd deal with it somehow.

But she knew that she'd never be able to accept Karen as her friend, too.

During dinner, the phone rang. Joe answered it, and then cupped a hand over it. "Karen, it's for you."

"Me?" Karen sounded surprised.

"Yes." Joe handed her the phone when she came over. "Someone called Jean."

Karen nodded, and took the phone. She talked in quiet tones into it for a moment, and then hung up. "Sorry about that," she apologized. "It's my aunt. She's in town for a convention, and wants to meet me tonight. I do hope that won't be a problem?"

"Of course not," Joe replied. "You're not chained to the house! Go out and enjoy yourself. It'll be the first time since you came."

"Yes," agreed Leslie slowly. "You don't seem to have any friends, or anything."

Karen shrugged. "I've not been here long enough to make any—except for Aggie. I'm not really one for the giddy social scene or singles bars, I'm afraid."

Leslie made a sympathetic noise. "Don't you ever want to meet a nice young man?" she asked.

"One day, definitely," Karen answered with a smile. "But right now, my job takes me all over the place. It's too flighty a life to have many long-term relationships. I mean, I'm here today and maybe next month . . ." Her voice trailed off as she caught sight of the expression on Aggie's face. Leslie saw it, too.

Aggie looked as if she'd been hit. "You're not thinking of going away, are you?" she asked, in a small, betrayed voice.

"No!" Karen exclaimed. "I would never leave you while you need me, Aggie. That's a promise. But . . . you have to realize that one day there might be another child who might need me more than you do. And if that day comes, I hope you'll be able to let me go and help her, too, like I've been helping you."

"No," Aggie said fiercely. "I won't let you go. I *won't*."

Leslie stared at her daughter in dismay. She'd felt quite relieved that Karen had made it perfectly clear that she was only here temporarily. But it didn't look as if Aggie wanted that to be true. She didn't want to lose Karen.

As Leslie had feared, Aggie had already bonded with her tutor. Perhaps Karen had even replaced Leslie in her daughter's affections. Leslie felt crushed, and, unfairly, bitter toward Karen once again.

Karen hurried through the darkening evening to the phone booth several blocks from the house. Outside it, on a bus bench, a tall, prim figure was seated. She rose to her feet as Karen approached, and then Karen embraced Jean warmly.

"Jean," she said, a little breathlessly. "I came as soon as I could without causing problems at the house. What are you doing here?"

"It's the trackers," Jean said bitterly. "I think they've found me. A man named Walsh. He was at the store today, asking about you and Lucy Hagen."

Karen went pale. She knew that if the trackers found her, she'd be lucky if all she got was a life sentence in some maximum security prison. And the idea of going to jail filled her with dread.

Still, that was the *best* thing that could happen to her if she was caught. Death was far more likely.

"Why didn't he grab you?" she asked. "Didn't he realize who you are?"

"I don't know," Jean admitted. She was pale and looked suddenly every minute of her age. "But I came to warn you, and to try to help you. We have to start closing things down before *they* do it for us. I don't know how long it will take him to find me, but I'd have to be a fool not to know he's got to be on my trail. And he's on yours, too. He has a photo of you from somewhere."

Karen scowled. "I never allow pictures of me to be taken," she said. "You know me better than that, Jean."

"He got one somehow," Jean answered, placing a hand on Karen's arm. "A telephoto lens. You couldn't have known. It isn't your fault. But it does mean that this will have to be your last one, at least for a while. Now they can identify you."

Karen didn't want to think about it. In days, her picture could be in every post office in the country. Even on *America's Most Wanted*. She could almost feel the prison walls closing in around her, and it scared her.

"About Aggie," Jean said, breaking into her bleak thoughts. "How is she?"

That brought a smile to Karen's face again. "Jean, she's the best I've ever seen. Her powers are still unfocused, but she's strong. Stronger than I am, stronger than anyone we've ever seen. She's really amazing. I haven't even started to discover just what she's capable of."

"Then it's as bad as I feared," Jean said coldly. "We don't have a moment to waste. We have to take her *now*."

"Now?" Karen echoed, shocked. "But she's nowhere near ready."

"That can't be helped," Jean insisted. "I want you to go back to the Travis house and kidnap her tonight."

CHAPTER 9

KAREN COULDN'T BELIEVE what Jean was asking her. ''If we take her now,'' she said slowly, ''she'll never really trust us. I need more time, to get her to believe in me. Please!''

''If that tracker finds us,'' Jean snapped, ''then there's *really* going to be trouble. You *know* what they'll do to us if we're caught.''

''Yes,'' agreed Karen, with dull pain. ''But, Jean—it's too soon! Aggie's doing well. I just need a little more time.''

A moment later, Jean gave a curt nod. ''All right. I'll give you two days, no more. Then, if you won't do it, I'll take her myself. We *have* to get her.''

''I know,'' Karen agreed with relief. ''Thank you.''

Jean started to move away. ''Keep your eyes open. If they've found me, they may find you.''

''Where will you be?'' Karen asked.

''Close by,'' Jean replied. ''Watching. You may need my

help. But it's best you don't know exactly where yet. Just in case.'' She turned, and strode away.

Watching her leave, Karen fingered her crystal nervously. Two days to get Aggie ready. Two days! It wasn't really enough, but she'd have to make it sufficient. It wasn't going to be easy. Underneath Aggie's surface hostility toward her parents, she really loved Joe and Leslie. Getting her to leave them was going to be quite a battle. . . .

In the morning, Aggie was having fun. Clutching her crystal, she sat on her bed, concentrating. She had seven of her stuffed animals flying about the room, whirling in and out in intricate patterns. Now that Karen had shown her how to do it, using her mind to levitate things was really easy. It was fun to play like this.

Karen had been right: using her special abilities had made them a whole lot less scary. The anger inside of her had died down a lot. It had been mostly frustration and fear, she realized, that had turned to anger. Now the frustration was gone and the fear was going. Aggie still knew that she wasn't quite normal. Other girls at school couldn't do what she could. But she was no longer alone; Karen was like her, and there were others, Karen had told her. She was special, not a freak.

And that felt good. Aggie had felt so terribly alone and lost before Karen had come. Now she felt wanted and needed. And, above all, believed. Karen never accused her of lying, like her parents did. At odd moments, Aggie wished that Karen were her older sister. That's what she felt like. Someone to trust, to believe in. Someone who helped her with all kinds of things.

The door opened, breaking Aggie's chain of thoughts. Karen's laugh came as she was showered with falling stuffed toys, as Aggie lost her mental grip on them.

''You're getting really good,'' Karen said, tossing the toys back at Aggie on the bed. Aggie "caught" them with her mind and sent them to their proper places on the shelves.

"I get kind of tired," Aggie admitted, slipping the crystal she'd been holding back into the neckline of her T-shirt. "But it's really fun. I can't wait to show Mom and Dad what I can do, and tell them what *really* happened to stuff around me."

Karen went down on her knees in front of Aggie, and gripped Aggie's hands. "Aggie," she said softly, "you really can't show your mom and dad what you can do. The power we have is a big secret. The biggest secret ever."

"Huh?" Aggie didn't understand. She had thought that the whole point of what they were doing together was so that she could explain everything to her parents, so that they would stop hating her and start loving her again. "Why?"

Karen slid to sit next to her and put an arm about her shoulders. "Because grown-ups can act like the children at your school. Even your mom and dad might. They *know* we're different from them, and that makes them scared of us. They're afraid that we might be able to make them do things. That we think that, because we have this power, we're *better* than them and want to control them. That makes them afraid of us, and when they get afraid, they get mean. Aggie, you're a smart girl. I know you can understand what I'm talking about."

Aggie didn't know what to say or think. She knew that Karen was right. If the kids at school could see what she could do, they wouldn't think it was fun. They'd be scared. And then they'd call her "freak" and pick on her even more. Just thinking about it brought the anger back again. "I don't want to be around people like that," she said. Would Mom and Dad be like that? Would they think she was a freak if they knew what she could do? Aggie didn't even want to think about that possibility.

Karen smiled down at her a little sorrowfully. "What if I

told you that there was a place where you could go away from those kinds of people?'' she asked gently. ''A special place where there were other girls who were just like you? It's where I live. We call it Sanctuary.''

Aggie frowned. ''You mean like a town?''

Karen shrugged. ''Sometimes it's in a town,'' she said. ''Sanctuary's more a kind of a group than a physical place. We move around to stay safe from people who want to hurt us. We teach each other, like I've been teaching you. And we protect each other. And when we're ready, we leave Sanctuary for a while and go to find other people like ourselves, people who need our help.'' She gazed down at Aggie. ''Would you like to go there with me?''

Aggie considered the idea. To be with other girls, ones who would be just like her. People who would think she was normal, and not a monster. It sounded terrific. ''Can I take my parents?'' she asked.

''No, Aggie,'' Karen replied sadly. ''Sanctuary isn't for them. They wouldn't like it there. They'd feel odd, left out.''

''If it's not for them,'' Aggie replied firmly, ''then it's not for me, either.'' She gazed back at Karen. ''I know I've had problems with my parents, but I know that they love me, deep down. And I love them, too. I'm not ready to leave them, not even for a place as wonderful as Sanctuary sounds.''

There was a knock on the bedroom door, and when Aggie called out, Joe poked his head in. ''Ready to go to the park, kiddo?'' he asked. ''Toss a few baskets?''

Aggie leaped from the bed, smiling happily. ''You bet!'' She half turned to Karen. ''You want to come, too?'' she asked.

Karen shook her head. ''No. You should spend some special time with your parents. I've got some thinking to do, anyway. I'll join you in a bit, okay?''

Shrugging, Aggie turned back to her father. ''Okay. Let's

go!'' she said enthusiastically. It felt so good to be back in control of her life again, thanks to Karen. Now she could get back together with her parents, and everything would be fine, just as it had always been. She didn't need any place called Sanctuary. She had everything she needed right here, at home. And she had no intention of losing any of it.

Walsh was seated in another rental car. He'd only had it three hours, and it was already starting to accumulate garbage. Taking a last sip of almost cold coffee, he tossed the cup into the fast-food leftovers and dialed a number on his car phone. As he waited for it to connect, he checked the laptop computer he'd brought with him. It showed a map of Eugene, and a pulsing, fuzzy light.

His backup answered the call. ''Walsh here,'' he said. ''I'm getting a good directional signal from the card. She's definitely here in the city. You take the van down Fourteenth, and we'll see if we can get a fix on her through triangulation. I think the time's come to pick up Jean Anderson for some serious questioning. She's obviously got an agent here in town, and we have to stop her before she gets another girl. I don't think we've got any time at all to spare.''

He hung up and tapped the laptop case impatiently. To the best of his knowledge, this wasn't how Jean behaved. She'd certainly not been a field agent for a long time. If she was here, now, it could only mean that she was trying to speed up the latest kidnapping. And he *had* to stop her in time.

''Hurry up,'' he muttered to himself. ''Hurry up. . . .''

It was fun, for once, at the park. Aggie was shooting hoops with her father, and Leslie was enjoying watching them. It seemed so wonderfully normal, something Leslie hadn't expected to see again for quite some time. Aggie's anger and resentment, and her continual brooding, seemed to have lightened from her shoulders. Leslie heard her voice being called, and she turned to see Karen hurrying over, smiling as always. Well, maybe that smile had proven to be infectious or something, because Aggie certainly seemed to have caught it.

"Hi," Karen said as she reached Leslie. She glanced at where Aggie was playing. "She's having a lot of fun, isn't she?"

"Yes," Leslie agreed, watching her daughter with affection. "She's like a new girl. Or, rather, the old Aggie back again. I almost hate to admit it, but you're a real miracle worker, Karen."

Karen shrugged. "No, I was just in the right place at the right time with the right training. She's simply outgrowing her problems, and coming to grips with who she is."

A ball flung by one of the other children went wild. It struck Aggie on the leg. Leslie's eyes narrowed as she saw Aggie whirl, the anger inside her quite evident. Leslie held her breath, wondering if her daughter was going to explode again and attack the boy who was glowering at her. It's what she would have done a week ago. But had she *really* changed?

The anger died down, and Aggie simply kicked the ball back to him. Then she returned to her own throw. Leslie breathed a sigh of relief. "I think she's really changing," she commented.

"She's trying," agreed Karen. "She still has the anger, but it's no longer in charge of her life. That's a good thing." She seemed to be staring off into the distance. "Uh, excuse me," she said apologetically. "Little girl's room." She gave a quick smile, and hurried off toward the public toilets.

Leslie turned back to watching her daughter at play. Aggie was laughing, weaving, and sometimes letting her father block her shots. It was so wonderful to be a *normal* family again!

* * *

Karen hurried over to where she had seen Jean standing. "Jean," she said, almost out of breath. "What are you doing here?"

The older woman was staring at Aggie, her hand on her crystal. "I told you I'd be watching," she replied. "She's still got a lot of anger."

"It's hard to get her to control it completely," Karen replied. "You know that. Look how long it took you with me."

Jean smiled fondly at her. "Yes, you were a tough one. But you came around, and now your own strength is in helping others do the same. You empathize with them because you were worse than most of them. Even Aggie."

It was odd thinking of those days. Karen had been eleven, just like Aggie. Only she didn't come from a loving family, like Leslie and Joe. Her father had abused her, and when the anger came, Karen had struck out furiously.

Her father had been in the hospital for six weeks, many of his blood vessels mysteriously ruptured. The police would have arrested her, Karen knew, if they could only have figured out how she could have done such a thing. Naturally, they couldn't, and she hadn't been able to tell them, either. She'd been placed in a group home, where she'd fought everyone.

And then she'd met Jean. . . .

"You haven't made a lot of progress with her," Jean commented, wrenching Karen's thoughts back to the present. "We need to go to Sanctuary immediately."

"I talked with her about it," Karen replied. "She doesn't want to go. Not without her parents. And there's no way we could take them, even if we wanted to."

Jean said snappishly, "I'm afraid with the trackers this close, we can't wait any longer. Whether she wants to come or not, we will have to take her and deal with the consequences as they arise."

"And we just forget about our rules?" asked Karen bitterly.

"Rules?" Suddenly Jean seemed to collapse in on herself, looking old and frail and tired. She turned haunted eyes on Karen. "Rules only work when both sides agree to them. The year before I rescued you, I found this little girl in Modesto, California. Her name was Joy. She was so smart, and so pretty. She wanted to be a ballerina, and she was able to focus so well that she could almost fly. I'll never forget how graceful she was when she danced, as if she were transported to another plane of existence.

"Joy loved her parents, and I was still young. I couldn't see why I should take her away from them, to separate them from one another. So I didn't. It seemed so harmless at the time. Her parents knew about Joy's special powers, and it didn't bother them. They loved her anyway.

"It didn't help when the trackers came. They took Joy from her loving parents under a court order. The next time I saw Joy was several years later, after they had finished testing her at one of their camps. When they were done, they *neutralized* her, so she wouldn't ever cause them any problems. That's just a polite word for electroshock. When she left that camp, she could barely walk, much less dance. Her mind was gone. They killed what made Joy special." Jean stared significantly at where Aggie was playing with her father. "I'll be waiting at the Burrard Motor Inn at the corner of Burrard and Third. Room twenty-three." She didn't look at Karen again.

Karen knew that there was nothing she could say to ease Jean's pain. So she turned and made her way back to the family. Aggie was squealing with laughter, almost matched by Joe's own bellows. Leslie's face was lit with pleasure.

They're a family again, Karen thought guiltily. *And now it's my job to wreck their happiness forever. . . .*

CHAPTER 10

THE PLAYING WENT on for another fifteen minutes, while Karen silently watched. Her emotions churned inside her, and she was afraid to even speak to Leslie. Surely the other woman would see the pain and guilt on her face if she tried. But Karen also knew that she had no choice. If the trackers found Aggie . . .

Gradually, she was able to get herself back under control again. Her own feelings no longer mattered. Even the feelings of Joe and Leslie and Aggie didn't matter. The only thing that was important now was to keep Aggie safe. To that end, Karen was prepared to lie without blushing and to trick and betray anyone she had to. Even Aggie herself.

''Enough!'' exclaimed Joe, collapsing onto the grass beside Leslie. He was smiling happily. ''I'm totally out of steam.''

''You're getting old,'' Leslie chided him, a smile on her lips.

''She's too young and too good for me,'' Joe protested.

"Aww," Aggie complained, not even winded. "Can't we stay here a little longer? Please? I'm not tired yet."

"Well, you ought to be," Joe complained, laughing. "You've exhausted me. I think it's time to drive home again."

"We can come back another day," Leslie added. "I think we'd better get back before your father collapses totally."

Joe clambered stiffly to his feet. "I need a nice, long bath," he said. "Soften these stiff muscles."

"I have an idea," Karen said quickly, stifling her shame at what she was about to do. "Why don't the two of you go ahead home and take that long bath? I'll walk back with Aggie, and burn off some of her energy."

"Yeah!" Aggie said enthusiastically. She was obviously not ready to head home yet. "Can we, Mom, huh?"

Leslie and Joe exchanged glances. Karen could see what they were thinking—a little quality time together without interruptions. . . . And, after all, what could possibly go wrong? Karen steeled her nerves, letting nothing show on her face. It had been hard enough taking Lucy Hagen, but she'd had the time to prepare Lucy. Aggie still didn't know what was going on, and had no idea that she would never see her parents again.

"Sure," Leslie said, with a wicked grin. "Sounds like a good idea."

Joe nodded. "We'll see you at the house, then, in about an hour."

"You got it," lied Karen.

Leslie bent to give her daughter a kiss, and then she and Joe headed for where they had parked the car. Karen couldn't look at them anymore, knowing how betrayed and confused and terrified they were going to start getting in an hour or so.

She led Aggie across the park, past a small duck pond. Aggie picked up a stone and tried to skim it across. It hit the water and sank. The next one, though, skipped right across the pond, and Karen knew that Aggie had nudged it with her mind. It was dangerous to do such things out in public, but Karen didn't have the heart right now to scold her.

"Karen," Aggie said abruptly, "how come you and I can do things that other people can't?"

Taking a deep breath, Karen answered, "You have something we call a Z chromosome. You know that chromosomes are what determines what sort of a person you are, don't you? Either a boy or a girl, tall or short, and all that sort of thing? The Z chromosome is very special. It's something that only women can have. And not even very many of them. Maybe one in a million, or even less. We don't really know. It's sort of a key to being able to focus."

Aggie nodded, and Karen hoped she was understanding this. It was something she usually spaced out over days, to make sure she was being understood. Now she had to tell it all quickly, and trust to Aggie's sharp mind to understand it all.

"You have this Z chromosome, too, don't you?" Aggie asked. "You can focus, too."

"Yes," agreed Karen. "But I'm not as good at it as you are, or as strong. And as you get older, the powers will get weaker. I'm not as strong now as I was when I was your age, though I'm still pretty good. And I wasn't as strong as you even when I was as young as you. You're very special, Aggie. I can't even begin to guess how strong you'll be when you're completely trained."

"How did it happen?" Aggie asked. "I mean, this chromosome thing."

Karen shrugged. "It just happened. We were born this way. Some men are born with an extra Y chromosome, and now some women are being born with a Z chromosome. Nature sometimes tries out new things to see what will happen. Many of them aren't very useful, and they disappear. Some of them linger and get stronger. The first of us appeared about fifty years ago, and there do seem to be more of us coming each year. Maybe in five hundred years everybody will have the Z chromosome.''

Aggie thought about this further. ''I don't know that I like being different from everyone else,'' she decided. ''Can't they just take it out of me?''

''No,'' Karen replied. ''It's far too small for that, and it's in every cell in your body. It's part of what makes you you. The only way to get rid of it would be to destroy you.'' She winced as she thought about Jean's story of Joy. ''Besides, I thought you were starting to like being able to do extra things?''

''I am, I guess,'' Aggie admitted. ''Now that I know I'm not the only one like this, I feel a lot better.'' She stared wistfully at a group of children playing together out on the grass. ''But I'm still on my own. I don't have any friends.''

''You have me,'' Karen said.

''Yeah, I know. But I meant friends of my own age.'' Her eyes narrowed and she glared at Karen. ''Besides, you said you weren't going to stay with us. How long *are* you going to stay?''

Karen shrugged. ''We'll see,'' she replied, trying not to wince at her evasion.

''That's no answer,'' Aggie grumbled. But she didn't seem to want to press it. She was probably afraid of the answer.

''Come on,'' Karen suggested. ''Let's go this way.'' She took Aggie's hand and led her away from the pond and toward Burrard Road.

It was time to begin the betrayal. Her stomach wrenched, but she knew she had no choice. She had to keep Aggie safe from the trackers. And Jean's room at the motel was the safest place for her right now. She couldn't afford to think about what Aggie would do and say when she realized that she could never go home again. . . .

Jean let herself into her motel room, fumbling her key as she was holding a paper bag filled with groceries. Just a few things for tonight and tomorrow that she'd picked up on the way back. She closed the door behind her and placed the groceries on the table by the door as she clicked on the light.

And almost died of shock.

Walsh was seated in the chair beside her small, neatly made bed. In his right hand, he held a gun that was pointed directly at her. In his eyes was a glint of satisfaction. "Hello, Jean," he murmured.

As soon as her heart had stopped pounding from the shock, Jean managed to blink and take a breath. She hadn't expected him this quickly. "You followed me?" she guessed.

"The business card I gave you," he said with a smug grin. "There's a transponder sandwiched inside it. A nice little gadget, and it enabled me to find you whenever I wanted you."

Jean sighed. That meant that others knew where she was, then. And they must have raided the bookstore, too. Thank goodness she'd told Ruth to clear out of there! Ruth and the others would be safe. They'd need to set up a new front, of course, but that could come later. Right now, she knew that she was in a terrible hole. "Then where are the others?" she asked.

"They'll be here shortly," Walsh replied. He was so smug now that he thought he had the upper hand. "I thought we'd have a little chat alone first." He gestured with the gun, and she followed his indications and sat down on the bed, her hands clasped in her lap where he could see them. "Maybe you can make this much less unpleasant than it could get and just tell me what I need to know. Otherwise it will have to get . . . messy.'' His eyes narrowed and he scowled at her. ''Where is Martha, or whatever her real name is? I know there's got to be another little girl involved. What's her name? Where is she?''

Jean couldn't afford to panic. He mustn't know that she'd ordered Karen to bring Aggie here as soon as possible. How long did she have? She didn't know. But she had to make certain that Walsh was gone by the time Karen arrived. If she still had her powers, that would be simple. But they'd worn out several years ago. She kept her crystal as a reminder of who she was now, not for any practical purpose.

Distract him, that was what she had to do. She stood up, ignoring the gun. He couldn't afford to shoot her—at least, not yet. He needed answers from her. She walked to where she had placed the bag of groceries. ''There are perishables in here,'' she informed him. ''Excuse me while I put them away.'' She carried the bag to the room's small kitchen area, and started to stack things in the fridge.

Walsh laughed incredulously. ''You carry neatness way too far, lady. You know that?''

''It's better than being like you,'' Jean answered. She gave him a disapproving stare. ''You really should try to smarten yourself up a little.''

''Give it up,'' Walsh advised her. ''I'm going to get the answers I want, Jean. We both know that. There are drugs that will turn your twisted mind inside out and make you beg to tell me what I want to hear. And if that doesn't work . . . well, at your age, your bones get really fragile, I understand. It would be very easy to break one or two until you're willing to answer me.''

''You enjoy this, don't you?'' she said in disgust.

''I predict that by the end of the day, we'll have your assistant kidnapper. And that little girl.'' His grin widened. ''And the one all-important thing: the location of Sanctuary.

We're going to have every last one of you in a camp by the end of the week."

Jean could stomach no more of his arrogance and lack of feeling. "Generations of women have been hunted and hounded by men like you," she spat. "Centuries ago, you called us witches and burned us at the stake. Nowadays you have more civilized words for it, but you still persecute and look to destroy us. I've seen my friends taken away and neutralized, just because we can do things that you can't. You're all so terribly afraid that you're going to be replaced, like modern-day Neanderthals. Evolutionary dead ends. Well, from the way you've been acting, that's exactly the fate you deserve. To become the dodo birds of the human race." She shook her head. "There have been times when I've wished that we were capable of fighting back, of hurting you and your kind as you've hurt us. But that's not our way. We won't stoop to your level." She gestured at the gun with a loaf of bread. "I'm not afraid of that. I'll die before I tell you anything."

Walsh looked at his gun and then laughed. "Oh, no, Jean. You're not going to die. I promise you that. You've got a whole lot of talking to do."

"Indeed?" Jean picked up a toilet roll, and brushed past him into the tiny bathroom. She set the roll down atop the toilet, and then poured herself a glass of water. She reached into her pocket and pulled out two small tablets and looked at them for a second. "No," she whispered. "You'll get nothing out of me, Walsh." She had a brief vision of Joy again, as she was the last time she'd seen her: eyes lifeless, body dragging, spirit murdered. No, that was not to be her fate. Anything but that! She steeled herself and then swallowed the tablets and washed them down with water. *You'll get nothing from me!* she thought savagely as the world evaporated around her.

* * *

Walsh was feeling very pleased with himself at that moment. Everything was falling right into place. He had everything he needed in his grasp. In just a few hours, everything would be over.

There was the crash of shattering glass from the bathroom, and then a loud thump. Suddenly worried, he jumped to the bathroom door. Jean was sprawled out on the floor amid shards of the broken glass. He bent over her, knowing what he would discover. There was no pulse. "Dammit," he muttered.

The door to the room slammed open, and two of his men burst in, guns at the ready. Frustrated and angry, Walsh straightened up.

"She took some kind of poison before I could stop her," he complained, irritated at having lost his head. "And I didn't get the girl's name!" To be so close, and yet end up with nothing! Maybe there was some kind of clue that she'd left? Something to tell him where this Martha or whatever-she-was-calling-herself was? He looked around the room, but everything was where it should be. There was nothing out of place. Damn her neatness! He could imagine that she'd even polished the phone.

The phone!

He snatched up the receiver, ignoring his men as they looked around the room. "Front desk?" he growled as a man's voice answered. "Do you keep records of all calls made from your rooms?"

"Yeah," the man answered. "But I'm not allowed to show them to anyone."

"You'll show them to me," Walsh said with satisfaction. "This is federal business. Either I see those records or you get to spend a few years in a small jail cell that's even rattier than this motel. I'll be right over." He slammed down the phone, and turned to his two men. "Both of you, let's go.

There's nothing left here.'' Ignoring the corpse in the bathroom, he led them at a trot toward the manager's office—and, hopefully, the answers he needed.

Karen led Aggie through the streets toward the motel. She felt sick at the terrible betrayal she was going to have to do, but she kept repeating to herself, over and over, that there was no other option. She had to keep Aggie safe. Even if it made Aggie hate her for it.

Aggie gave her a lopsided stare. ''What are you going to be when you grow up?'' she asked.

Karen couldn't help laughing at that. ''I'm already grown up,'' she answered.

''No, I mean when you're really old,'' Aggie explained. ''Like thirty.''

Smiling, Karen said, ''I always wanted to help people. And that's what I'm doing, helping people like you, Aggie. Just as somebody once helped me. What about you? What do you want to be?''

''A mountain climber,'' Aggie replied promptly.

''I don't think there's much money in that,'' Karen joked. But she knew what Aggie meant. ''You want to be alone, don't you? So did I. But you can't.''

Aggie studied her for a moment. ''What would you like me to be?'' she asked. ''Someone like you, who helps people?''

''If that's what you want, Aggie,'' Karen replied. ''What's important is what *you* want to be. You need to have a vision for yourself. It would be wonderful if you wanted to help other young girls like you. But if you'd rather be something else—even a mountain climber!—then you should go for it.'' The irony of what she was saying wasn't lost on her. She was telling Aggie to be whatever she wanted, and yet she was planning to kidnap her and take her away from everything she wanted. . . .

Aggie suddenly looked around, puzzled. "This isn't the way home," she objected.

"I know," agreed Karen easily. "I just wanted to stop in here really quickly and see a friend." She gestured at the motor inn they had just reached. "Do you remember me telling you that someone once helped me, just like I helped you? Well, she's staying here, and I wanted to stop in and say hello. You don't mind, do you?"

Aggie shrugged; it obviously didn't matter to her. Yet. Karen led the way into the parking lot, and then glanced around, looking for room 23. Following the numbers, she walked along the pavement, and then stopped at the right door. She knocked, and waited. There was no reply, which puzzled her. She rapped again, and then frowned. There wasn't even a sound from inside.

"That's odd," she murmured. Jean should definitely be here; she had been very clear in her instructions. She tried the door, but it was locked. Worried now, Karen fished the crystal out of her blouse and focused on the door lock through it. She could feel the tumblers move with her mind, and the door clicked. Karen pushed the door open, and called out, "Jean!" Could she just be sleeping? But she wouldn't do that, not when she was expecting to have to flee with Aggie.

Everything looked fine, but Karen had an itch in her mind that told her the room stank of trouble. She turned to Aggie. "You wait here," she ordered. "I'm just going to take a look for a minute." Then she moved into the room, the crystal clutched tightly in her fist, her mind probing for any sign of anything at all. There didn't seem to be any living person here. Not Jean, and, thankfully, not the trackers.

She moved through the room, and then she saw the bathroom door ajar. Crossing to it, she gasped in shock.

Jean's body lay sprawled on the floor, her eyes sightless, her face calm. There was a catch in Karen's throat as she stared down at her mentor and friend, knowing she was dead. Sadness started to grow inside her, along with fear.

And then Aggie, just behind her, screamed. Karen whirled around, shocked and dismayed that the girl should have seen this. She hadn't even realized that Aggie had followed her into the room.

Aggie whirled and ran for the door in panic.

"Aggie!" Karen cried. "Come back here!"

The door flew shut behind Aggie, without her touching it. Karen grabbed the handle but pulled her hand back immediately. The handle was red-hot. She stared in disbelief as it slowly melted out of shape, jamming the door shut.

Karen had had no idea that Aggie was capable of such a feat. She'd realized that Karen could simply unlock the door, so she had rendered the door useless by melting the lock. Her power was truly astonishing. There was no telling what she could do.

And, given her state of panic right now, there was no telling what she *might* do. Aggie wasn't thinking straight; she'd acted from shock and fear when she'd seen Jean's body. Now she was probably running straight home, and had locked the only person who could help her in a motel room with a dead body.

Now what was Karen going to do?

CHAPTER 11

"THERE WERE NO calls from room twenty-three?" Walsh growled at the manager.

"None at all." He was a grubby little man, a fat stomach bulging over his belt, his hair restricted to a small area about each ear. "She booked in yesterday at four, and paid for three days. That's all she did, as far as I know."

"Damn." Walsh turned away, thinking furiously. He was pretty certain that the freaks couldn't do mind-to-mind stuff. Telepathy, that was it. At least none of the ones he'd ever caught could. And, anyway, the powers got very thin as the women got older. Whatever Jean Anderson might have been able to do as a young woman, she was almost powerless when she died. Otherwise she wouldn't have needed to kill herself. So she would have had to talk to this Martha girl on the phone. But if not from her room, then where?

Of course! She was covering her tracks, just in case. He turned back to the manager. "Where's the nearest public phone?" he demanded.

The greasy man thought a minute. ''On the corner, by the bus stop.''

Walsh walked out, and moved briskly to the phone. He read the number, and then hurried to his car and dialed Selma. When she answered, he snapped, ''Find out what calls were made from a public phone here in Eugene.'' He gave her the number. ''From after four yesterday to about an hour ago. It'll be somewhere local. Call me back when you have an answer.''

Impatiently, he waited, wondering how long the search would take. His eyes flickered over the people who passed by. Was one of them the girl Martha? Or maybe that young kid that ran along was the girl they were all seeking? There was no way to tell without help.

It was only about five minutes before the phone rang, and Walsh scooped it up.

''Only three calls,'' Selma told him. ''One was to a bar, one out of town. The last was a house belonging to a Joseph Travis.'' She gave him the address, which he scribbled in his notebook. Then he sounded his horn. One of his men—he could never remember their names—came over. He showed the man the address. ''I'm heading over there now,'' he said. ''I don't want to worry the family, so you stay behind. I'll call if I need backup, okay?'' He assumed it was. Without waiting for a reply, he pulled out of the parking lot.

As he'd figured, the motel wasn't very far from the house. It took him ten minutes to reach the place. A nice Tudor style, very suburban. Professional people, which meant they would be intimidated by authority. Everything was going perfectly. He could feel in his bones that he was on the right track. Everything was coming together nicely.

Walsh ambled up the path and rang the bell. After a moment, it was answered by a man in his midthirties. Over his shoulder, Walsh could see a woman watching. "Mr. and Mrs. Joseph Travis?" he asked politely.

"Yes," said the man. He frowned slightly. "Who are you?"

He hauled out his wallet and opened it to his ID card, which he flashed in Travis's face. "Special Agent Walsh," he explained. "May I come in? I'd like to see your daughter."

"Our daughter?" Travis echoed, moving back to allow him to enter.

"She's not here right now," the mother said, worry and concern in her voice. "Why? Did she do something wrong? Or has something happened to her?"

"She's with her tutor," Travis explained, just as pale and uncertain as his wife. "What's wrong?"

Keeping them on edge was the best thing to do; this way they'd cooperate fully. Walsh fished the slightly battered picture of Martha out of his pocket and showed it to them. "Is this the girl? Is her name Martha?"

Mrs. Travis examined the photo with confusion. "That's her. But her name's Karen."

"That may be the name she's using now, yes." Walsh started to look about the room, without asking permission. If the girl was with this Karen, then that could mean trouble. The girl he could ignore; she'd be too inexperienced with her powers to be any trouble. But Karen was another matter entirely. She was only in her midtwenties and no doubt very experienced. She could do all kinds of things, if she got the chance. He'd have to see to it that she didn't get the opportunity.

"What's going on?" the girl's mother demanded. "What has she done? Is she in some sort of trouble? And why did you call her Martha?"

Walsh ignored the questions for a moment, to allow them to fester in the parents' minds. The more worried they were, the better. "Did this Karen give your daughter a gift?" he demanded.

"A gift?" Travis shrugged. "Well, I guess."

"A crystal on a neck chain?" Walsh prompted.

Mrs. Travis frowned. "How could you know that?"

Walsh gave her a weary smile. He'd practiced it for a long time. It seemed to say that he knew a lot and could help. "My agency knows a great deal about this girl who's calling herself Karen today. She kidnaps children."

"Kidnaps?" Travis had gone pale as what Walsh was saying sank in. "And she's alone with Aggie. . . ." Abruptly he ran to the door. "They're walking home from the park. I'm going after them. If she's done anything to Aggie, anything at all . . ." His voice trailed off, but there was cold fury in his eyes.

Perfect, thought Walsh. Travis would keep Karen busy while Walsh could go for the girl. This was working out really well.

Travis flung open the door, and then all three of them reacted with astonishment.

Aggie was standing there, tears streaming down her face. She was shaking.

Mrs. Travis brushed past Walsh and scooped her daughter into a tight embrace. "Aggie!" she exclaimed, relieved, and crying almost as much as her daughter. "My God, Aggie, are you okay?"

The father joined them. "We were really scared for you, honey. Is everything fine?"

The girl didn't speak, but her tears seemed to be lessening. She gave a strangled sob, and then a loud sniff. Travis handed her a tissue and she blew her nose.

Walsh joined them in the doorway, relieved. Not only was the girl here, but she was alone! No sign of Karen to cause trouble. "Hello, Aggie," he said gently, so as not to scare her. "My name is Walsh. Can you tell me where Karen is?"

The girl blinked and then looked at him, her eyes filled with unshed tears. ''I left her at the other place.''

''The other place?'' asked Walsh, confused. ''What other place?''

''I don't really know,'' Aggie answered. ''Some sort of motel.''

Walsh almost screamed with frustration. *They'd gone to Jean Anderson's room!* He could only have missed them both by minutes! What an idiot he was. If he'd only stayed there, he'd have had them both by now without having to involve the parents at all. But if Karen was still there . . . He had to call his men. ''Can I use the phone?'' he demanded. They'd be able to get Karen with a tranquilizer gun before she could cause any trouble.

The Travises were too happy to have their daughter back safely to care. ''Over there,'' the father said.

Walsh located it, and dialed the van's cellular. ''The girl's at the motel room,'' he snapped. ''Get in there and secure her, fast, before she can get away.'' Then he turned back to the family. ''Now, Aggie,'' he began.

''That's enough questions,'' Mrs. Travis said firmly. ''We have our daughter back, and we're certainly not going to allow her to go off again with Karen. We can call the police and let them take over now.''

''Police?'' Aggie asked, frightened. ''Mom, what's going on? What's Karen done?''

Walsh was starting to get frustrated with these people and the way they were arguing. Still, that was because they couldn't see the larger picture. ''I'm sorry,'' he said firmly, ''but I will need Aggie's help. Maybe when she's calmed down I could take her down to our office, and—''

''She's not going anywhere,'' Travis said firmly. ''She's home now, and she's staying home.''

Walsh felt like hitting the idiot. "You don't understand how important this is!"

"No," agreed the father. "I don't. But I know how important *Aggie* is, and that's all I'm concerned about right now. Her safety means more than anything you might want her for. So maybe it's about time you started explaining to us just what this is all about?"

Taking a deep breath and struggling to control his temper, Walsh nodded. "All right. There is a group of people at loose in this country that are very, very dangerous. My section . . . finds those people."

"Finds them?" Travis echoed. "What do you mean? How are they dangerous? Are they terrorists, or what? And what does this have to do with Aggie?"

"These people are dangerous because they're *different*," Walsh explained, trying to be patient. For now, he needed their cooperation. He didn't want to be forced to leave to obtain a warrant and then come back. There was no telling what might happen in the meantime. "They prey on innocent young girls. They snatch them away from their families, who never get to see their daughters again. These people are dangerous because they can't be controlled and they're very difficult to stop. They don't follow any of our laws—"

"Laws," said a woman's voice from behind him, "that let people like *you* hunt children like Aggie."

Walsh whirled around and saw that it was the Martha/Karen girl. She was breathing heavily, obviously having run here from the motel.

Karen flashed a smile at Aggie. "The lock was a good idea," she said approvingly. "But you forgot about the window." Then she turned back to face Walsh again.

He took an involuntary step back on seeing the savagery in her eyes. His throat went dry as he realized she was holding her crystal at the ready. He, of all people, knew only too well what she was capable of.

"I think it's time for the truth," she said simply.

"Truth?" Mrs. Travis scowled. "Karen, he's told us some terrible things about you." She was clutching Aggie to her protectively. "That you kidnap children. That you're an outlaw." She shook her head. "Is he right?"

"Yes," Karen admitted. "Everything he's told you is true."

Aggie stared at the young woman in shock. She'd run from the motel room because she had been scared. She'd never seen anyone dead before, and it had just been so hard. The Voice had been almost screaming at her, and she'd panicked. Then she'd run all the way home. Now Mom and Dad were protecting her. It felt so wonderful, knowing that they loved her and would look after her. But she hadn't really been scared of *Karen.* It had just been the dead person and everything. And the Voice had been so scared.

She had heard everything that Walsh had said about Karen, but she hadn't really believed it. Karen was her friend, and she would never do anything like the things he had said she did. But now Aggie with her own ears had heard Karen admit that she was a criminal and a kidnapper. She still couldn't really believe it. "I thought you were my friend," she said in a small, hurt voice. "You wouldn't *really* have kidnapped me, would you?"

Karen looked back at her, and Aggie was puzzled. Karen actually looked happy, which made no sense. Especially when she answered the question. "Yes," she said. "Aggie, I'm not going to lie to you. I took you to the motel intending to kidnap you."

"Why, you—" her father began, starting forward, but Karen held up her hand.

"I know it sounds bad," she said. "And I didn't want to do it. But I would have." She glanced at Walsh. "You see, everything he's told you is the truth. I *do* kidnap young girls. I *do* belong to a group who break the law. And there's a very good reason that I do both of those things." She glared at Walsh as if daring him to try to shut her up.

"There is this group of people in the government," she continued, talking to Aggie and her parents. "Years ago, they discovered that some girls are born . . . *different*." She smiled at Aggie. "It's what I started to tell you earlier. We have this odd chromosome which makes us unusual. The government discovered this about thirty years ago. They started to study people like me. And like Aggie. They discovered that there was something different about our minds that enabled us to affect things around us directly with our thoughts. The government thought this would be something useful to have, a new kind of weapon that they could have in their arsenal, one that no other country would have. But then there was a problem. You see, we don't like hurting other people. They found that their *weapons* were useless to them. Worse, that they were a threat.

"You see, so far no man has developed these powers of ours. And, as you know, most of the people in the military are men. They started to worry about us. They believed that we could do things that we couldn't."

"Time out," Travis said firmly. "Karen, what you and Walsh are talking about is ludicrous. It can't exist. I don't know what you're doing or why, but this story of yours is crazy."

"It's not crazy," Karen said gently. "Hard to accept, yes. But it's true." Her eyes flickered, and Aggie realized that she was looking for something to convince her parents. "Take a look at the telephone."

Aggie stared at it, knowing what Karen had in mind. The

receiver lifted off the cradle, and floated upward about a foot. It jiggled in the air, and then settled back into place. Aggie's mother went tense and started to shake.

"That's what we're talking about," Karen explained quietly.

"But what's that got to do with Aggie?" demanded Leslie, holding on to Aggie tightly.

"Aggie's like me," Karen replied. "She can do what I can do. That's why Walsh is after her. You see, he and the people like him see us as a threat."

Walsh growled low in his throat, and then pulled a gun from a hidden shoulder holster. "You *are* a threat!" He started to aim the gun at Karen.

He didn't get far. The gun leaped to life in his hands, slamming hard against the wall. He gave a cry of pain. The gun slammed again as Karen tried to force him to drop it.

It was too much for Aggie's father. He jumped forward, and grabbed at Karen's arm. Karen was distracted, and cried out. She lost her focus on Walsh, who grinned nastily and jumped for her. With his left hand, he ripped the crystal from around her neck and flung it aside. His right hand brought the pistol up to her temple.

Aggie's father fell back, shocked by the sudden violence and unsure of what was happening, and whose side he should be on. *He means well*, the Voice told Aggie, *but he's very confused*.

He wasn't the only one. Aggie didn't know quite what was going on either. She watched, too confused to know what to do.

"See what I mean?" growled Walsh, keeping the gun to Karen's head. "You can't trust her kind at all."

"Then . . . then it's all true?" asked Aggie's mother. She was clearly very bewildered.

"It's true," agreed Walsh. "Just not the way she's telling

it. These women have banded together, ignoring the needs of our country, and they've hidden themselves away. They're growing stronger, as they find more and more like themselves. They indoctrinate them, make them believe that they're superior to normal human beings. That they should rule us. They're waiting, building their strength up, and then they'll take over. It's only my department that stands between them and the end of the human race.''

Karen snorted. ''Listen to him!'' she cried. ''He's so crazed with fear. He's inventing excuses for what he does to people like me. Ask him what will happen to Aggie if he gets his hands on her. Ask him! And he *will* get her, if I don't help her. The courts are on his side. The government is on his side. They're as scared of us as he is. They'll let him take her. And you know what he'll do to her?''

''Shut up!'' Walsh snarled, his finger tightening on the trigger. Then he turned to Aggie's parents. ''Don't listen to her,'' he begged them. ''She's lying. She'll say anything to try to win you over to her side.''

''He'll give her a lobotomy,'' Karen said, heedless of her peril. ''Because they can't allow her to stay the way she is. She terrifies them. They'll try to cut out what makes her special. And the only way they can do that is by wiping her mind of every rational thought. If he gets hold of Aggie, he'll turn her into a drooling vegetable. Why do you think I came back? He killed the best friend I ever had. She poisoned herself rather than be taken by him to be questioned and then have her mind wiped. I knew he'd be here, waiting for me. The only reason I came here is because I care about Aggie.''

Aggie could see that her parents didn't know whom or what to believe. This was all too much for them. She was still very confused herself. But she had to know the truth. She really wanted to believe Karen because she liked her. And she didn't like Walsh. But Aggie knew that this didn't mean that Karen was right and Walsh was wrong. She *had* to know the difference.

And there was only one way that she could think of to know it: the Voice. *Wake up*, she told it. *I need your help.*

I know, the Voice replied. *But I can't tell you what Karen is thinking. She's like you. She can control her mind. I can't get past her barriers.*

Talk to her, Aggie said. *Maybe she'll let you in.*

The Voice gave the mental equivalent of a shrug. And then it tried.

Aggie almost collapsed from the shock. She heard, inside her mind, Karen's voice even though she didn't open her mouth to speak. *Aggie? Is that you? Are you speaking directly to my mind? That's astonishing! I don't know anyone else who can do it.*

It's not me, Aggie thought back to her. *It's the Voice. It's doing this.*

No, Karen said firmly. *The Voice is really you. You're just pretending it isn't because it scares you. Do what you must.*

I can't read your thoughts, Aggie told her. *You're strong enough to block me.*

I don't mean to, Karen answered. *Try now.*

Aggie did, and suddenly her brain was on fire.

It was as if she *was* Karen for a moment. Or for a lifetime. She could see into Karen's memories, and into every last mental nook and cranny. She saw Karen's childhood, how her father had mistreated her and abused her. How Karen had accidentally hurt him. How Jean had saved Karen, and then shown her how to control the anger.

She saw the truth.

And then she was back in her own mind again, shaking with what she had seen. There were now no secrets at all between her and Karen.

And Karen had been telling the absolute truth about everything.

While all of this had been going on, neither her parents nor Walsh had been aware of anything. They were still arguing about who was right and wrong.

"She's lying," Walsh said.

Aggie could feel her mother's confusion. "One of you is," she agreed. But she didn't know which one.

"Leslie," Karen said urgently, "Aggie has the power to do things. Great things. It's something she was born with, something they want to take away from her because they're afraid of it."

"Shut up!" Walsh snarled, his patience at an end. He slammed the pistol against her head, making Karen cry out.

"No," Aggie's father said, his eyes narrowing as he watched Karen almost buckle under the blow. "*You* shut up. You say that *she's* the criminal, but you're the one doing the strong-arm tactics, not her. She's trying to talk, and you're beating her."

"You idiot!" Walsh growled. "I'm trying to save us from them. We're on the same side, only you're too stupid to realize it. This witch is trying to make your daughter into one of them, and I'm trying to save her. And the rest of the human race."

Aggie could feel the waves of confusion from both of her parents. They didn't know what to believe. They had been trained to accept that people who worked for the government were the good guys, and they wanted to believe Walsh. But they could see what he was doing to Karen. There was a welt across her head where he'd hit her with the gun. And they had liked Karen. But if she really wanted to kidnap their daughter, how could they trust her? It was all too much for them, and they simply couldn't decide.

They couldn't. But Aggie could. She had seen the truth,

and she knew that Karen was right. She clutched her crystal.

Walsh saw her do this, and alarm crossed his face. He whirled his hand around, the gun coming to bear on Aggie as his finger tightened on the trigger.

CHAPTER 12

AGGIE WAS CONCENTRATING her thoughts as never before now. She was vaguely aware of her father giving a cry of rage and jumping toward Walsh. She half saw Walsh club him with the butt of his gun and then concentrate back on her again. Aggie could read Walsh's thoughts now, and they were repulsive.

I have to stop her! he was thinking frantically. *She's a monster, and she's got to be killed. She's even more uncontrollable than the rest!*

Aggie smiled grimly to herself; he didn't know the half of it! She *was* stronger than Karen. She knew that from having shared Karen's thoughts. And she knew that there was nothing that Walsh could do to stop her.

She allowed him to continue to struggle with the gun. He was trying to pull the trigger, to shoot and kill her. But she controlled his finger, and she set it as rigidly as a rock, refusing to let it move. Sweat was beading on his forehead and trickling down his face, and she could almost taste the fear in his stomach as he realized what was happening.

And that was only the beginning of it. Unlike Karen, Walsh couldn't hide a single thought from her. She could peel away all his glib excuses and read what he was *really* like. Just as Karen had claimed, he was fueled by fear and hatred. He saw the women with their powers as a threat to himself and everyone else like him. They were different, so they had to be stopped for the good of the human race. But even that wasn't a pure thought.

He wasn't simply trying to save mankind as he knew it from the next phase of evolution. He *enjoyed* what he did. The women made him feel inferior, and the way he compensated for it, the way he made himself feel big and in control again, was to hurt them. She could see his memories, and they disgusted Aggie. She could see him taking a young, precocious girl of nine and hurting her, forcing her to use her powers, and then drugging her. When she was quiet, he had ordered an operation on her brain that stopped all her abilities. And they wrecked her personality, too.

And Walsh had *enjoyed* it. He'd felt glad when he saw the little girl suffering, because he thought she *deserved* to suffer, just because she was different from him. And that hadn't been just one isolated case. He'd done it to many, many people.

And he still wanted to do it. He wanted to examine Karen and Aggie, and then take a knife to their brains, to destroy them. Or, failing that, just to kill them. He wanted to find out where Sanctuary was, so that he could wipe out everyone who lived there. He wanted to remove everyone from the planet that had the Z chromosome. He tried to pretend it was because these women were evil, and he was keeping the human race pure. But, deep inside, he was doing it because they scared him, and made him feel inferior. And because it meant that he could do terrible things to people and it was his job. He would get paid and praised for hurting and killing helpless girls and women. He *enjoyed* doing it.

Aggie was totally disgusted by what she could see in his mind. And after the disgust came the anger. Anger like she'd never known before. She had seen what this man had done, and what he would do again if she ever let him go. She would be one of his victims, and Karen, too. She could see him, watching Jean die. He didn't feel sad when she died, just furious that she'd escaped him without telling him what he'd wanted to know. If he could have, he'd have killed her over again for that. Since he couldn't, he aimed to take it out on Karen instead. He'd make her suffer for what Jean had done.

There was no containing her anger now. It was bad enough that Walsh had wanted to hurt her, but he was still planning all the sick and twisted things he would do to hurt Karen. And Karen had walked into a trap simply because she cared so much about Aggie. She had risked her own life to save Aggie. And Aggie wasn't going to let him hurt Karen. Or anyone else, ever again.

The anger flowed through her, giving her strength that she had never realized she had. The whole room seemed to explode in shades of light. She could see the aura about Walsh, and those around her parents and Karen, too. Karen's glowed brightly, much stronger than the others. It had to be because she knew how to use it. Aggie supposed that her own looked like this to Karen, too.

Walsh's halo of light was dark, with blacks and purples running through it. It was a manifestation of the anger and hatred inside him. Reaching out with her powers, Aggie grabbed this darkness about Walsh and threw him against the wall. He cried out as he hit, and the gun went spinning away. Aggie ignored it, focusing in on the man. Her fury raged out of control, and she unleashed it all on him.

He began to rise from the floor, still plastered firmly against the wall. His veins were bulging, his eyes bugging. He gasped for breath, and struggled futilely to escape. Aggie had seen in Karen's mind how Karen had stopped her own father when he had attacked her. And Aggie had understood what Karen had done, and how she, too, could do it. She could reach out with her mind and just squeeze Walsh's heart and make it stop. It would be the simplest thing in the world to do, and then his hatred would be gone. She could hear him choking, gasping for breath, but it didn't bother her. It was no more than he deserved.

Her parents were huddled together, watching what was happening without understanding any of it. But Karen understood. She grabbed hold of Aggie's arm.

"No, Aggie!" she cried. "Don't kill him."

Aggie frowned, puzzled. She kept her grip on Walsh, enjoying seeing him struggle, but looked at Karen. "Why not?" she demanded. "He hurt you. He wants to hurt you even more. He wants to kill me. And he's hurt and killed so many other people. He deserves to die."

"Aggie," Karen said, trying hard to explain, "I tried to teach you never to use your powers to hurt *anyone*. Not even him." She gestured at the gasping man stuck halfway up the hallway wall. "If you kill him, then you'll be as bad as he is. He's the one who thinks he has the right to hurt and kill, and you *know* that's wrong. So if you hurt and kill him, you'll be doing something that you know is wrong. It might feel good now, but it won't when your anger goes away. You'll be disgusted with yourself, because you'll have started to become like him. Aggie, please—let him go."

Aggie wasn't sure she quite followed all of that, but she knew that Karen firmly believed it. She hesitated. Walsh didn't deserve to live: that she was sure of. But . . . if *she* killed him, maybe it *would* make her as bad as him. And she didn't ever want to become anything as disgusting as that.

She stopped her attack on him, and let him slide down the wall to the floor. His veins returned to normal, and he drew in a long, whooping gasp of air. After considering the matter for a moment, Aggie reached out with her mind again, and moved into his. It was like trying to walk in a sewer, all icky and disgusting. But she knew what she was doing this time, and it only took a few moments. Then she pulled out and let him go completely.

Walsh collapsed to the floor, still wheezing a little, but otherwise unharmed. Karen gasped and ran to him.

"Don't worry," Aggie said. "I didn't kill him."

Karen bent to help Walsh up. He looked at her in confusion, but accepted her hand. His eyes looked around the hallway, seeing everyone, but understanding none of it.

"What's going on?" he asked. His voice was gentle, and there was none of the hatred in it. "Who are you people?"

Aggie smiled slightly. "I'm Aggie Travis," she told him. "What's your name?"

He had to work hard at that one. His mouth opened and closed, and then he smiled. "Terry!" he said triumphantly. "Terry Walsh."

"Hello," Aggie said, smiling.

"Hello," he said back, with a returned smile just as bright as hers.

Aggie's mother moved forward, and stared at Walsh. "Aggie," she asked in a quiet, shocked voice, "what have you done?"

She shrugged. "I erased all the bad parts in his mind. I didn't take away his personality, but all his hatred and fear and all the memories of what he's done to people like me are gone. He'll be much nicer from now on. And much safer."

Karen looked surprised, but she didn't say anything. She knew that this was better than killing Walsh, but she obviously still didn't like it a lot. Tough. Karen was a lovely person, but she didn't realize that sometimes you had to fight back in some way. And this was one that only Aggie could do. The young woman turned and walked out of the house, staring down the street.

"There will be others like Walsh here soon," she said sadly. "He had two other agents working with him at the motel. I only just avoided them. They'll track him here next. And there will be others after them." She turned around. "All you've done, Aggie, is bought us a short respite."

Leslie moved forward and put an arm around Aggie's shoulders. She gave Karen a nervous smile. "Then you'll have to go," she said simply. "They mustn't catch you here."

Karen's face was hard, but her eyes were sympathetic as she said, "I have to take Aggie with me."

"What?" Aggie's father demanded. "You can't take her!"

Karen sighed. "You have to believe me," she said gently, "that I'd have done anything I could to change this. All I want is for Aggie to grow up with people who love her. I know you and Leslie do, Joe, but it's not that simple. You've seen what she's like. What she can do."

"No," Joe said, holding on to Aggie tightly. "You can't take her. We love her!"

Leslie shook her head. "Joe, I hate to say this, but Karen's right. You saw what happened. There's a man in our hallway who was going to take Aggie away and dissect her like a frog because he was afraid of her powers. And there are more like him out there. Right now, they have the law on their side, so we wouldn't be able to stop them."

"I could stop them," Aggie said with confidence.

"You have to sleep sometime," Karen replied. "And they have tranquilizer guns that will stop you before you're even aware of them. You can't fight these people on your own, Aggie. You *need* to be with people like yourself."

"Yes," Aggie's mother agreed. "Karen's right. She *has* to go with Karen."

"No." Aggie's father was still refusing to believe it. "They won't take her. We'll hide her. We can change our names, move away . . ."

"They'll find you," Karen said with absolute conviction. "They are utterly intent on destroying us, Joe. If you keep Aggie with you, sooner or later they will find her. And then they will destroy her mind. And then, if she's lucky, they'll kill her."

Leslie turned to her husband. "Joe," she said gently, "This isn't our choice any longer. It's Aggie's. It's her life they're after. She has to make her own decision." She turned back to Aggie, who could see her mother's eyes shimmering with tears. "What do *you* think you should do, Aggie?"

It all came down to this. Aggie was being torn by conflicting emotions. She loved her mother and father very much, and she wanted to be with them so much it hurt. But Karen was right: Walsh's partners would find her, sooner or later. She needed help, she needed training, and she needed her parents not to be in danger because of her. Walsh would have killed her father to get at her, and the next agent might succeed where Walsh had failed.

Aggie looked at her parents, and was aware that there were tears on her own face. She hadn't realized that she was crying. "I have to go with Karen," she said softly, trying not to choke up. "I have to be safe, and I can't let them hurt you both to get to me. I don't want to go, but it's the only choice I can make."

Joe nodded slowly, understanding at last. He gave her a hug that he didn't want to end. "You'll always be my little girl," he told her, choking up. "Promise you'll come back someday soon."

How could she do that? She knew that the agency's men

would be watching her parents for any sign of anything like that. "I love you, Dad," she said, not answering his demand.

Then her mother hugged her. "Where will you take her?" she asked Karen.

Karen shook her head. "I can't tell you," she replied. "It's better for everyone if you don't know. For now, we have to stay hidden. But maybe one day . . ." She reached out and put an arm around Aggie's shoulder. "I promise you both that I'll take very good care of her."

Aggie walked slowly away from the house with Karen. The young woman gestured to Walsh's car. "I don't think he'll mind us borrowing it," she murmured. Aggie nodded, and clambered into the passenger seat, kicking aside the mess.

She had to fight really hard to avoid looking back as Karen drove her down the street and into a brand-new life.

EPILOGUE

SOME WARS ARE *fought very quickly, over in days. Some take years. The wars of evolution, though, can take many years. It may be many generations before they're over. Changes come from smaller battles, and some last only moments. A strange new chromosome in a young girl's body has led to another battle in an ongoing war.*

It is a war that won't end anytime soon, because it is a war being fought against fear and hatred and suspicion. Some people see this new race of humans as a threat to the old. They won't go quietly into extinction, and would prefer to kill the new. And the new race must hide and fight for its own survival, passing on its strange powers to its children, and teaching them how to control their abilities.

Ten thousand years from now, perhaps there will be an

entire new race of people with powers like Aggie's. And they may look back at this time and realize that here was a turning point.

Here is where their new race began.